Object of Lust
By Charles Runyon

Writing as Mark West

Black Gat Books • Eureka California

OBJECT OF LUST

Published by Black Gat Books
A division of Stark House Press
1315 H Street
Eureka, CA 95501, USA
griffinskye3@sbcglobal.net
www.starkhousepress.com

OBJECT OF LUST
Published and copyright © 1962 by Softcover Library, Inc.
New York, as by "Mark West."

All rights reserved under International and Pan-American
Copyright Conventions.

ISBN: 979-8-88601-018-3

Cover design by Jeff Vorzimmer, ¡caliente!design, Austin, Texas
Text design by Mark Shepard, shepgraphics.com
Cover art by Ernest Chiriacka

PUBLISHER'S NOTE:
This is a work of fiction. Names, characters, places and
incidents are either the products of the author's imagination or
used fictionally, and any resemblance to actual persons, living
or dead, events or locales, is entirely coincidental.
Without limiting the rights under copyright reserved above, no
part of this publication may be reproduced, stored, or
introduced into a retrieval system or transmitted in any form
or by any means (electronic, mechanical, photocopying,
recording or otherwise) without the prior written permission of
both the copyright owner and the above publisher of the book.

First Stark House Press/Black Gat Edition: February 2023

"Charles Runyon wrote some of the most innovative and powerful paperback originals in the 1960s and 1970s. As a former crime reporter, his books have a savage reality; as a fiction writer, he is both grim and lyrical by turns. He deserves major rediscovery."
—Ed Gorman

"There was one I wrote under the nom de plume of Mark West, which was published under the unforgettable title: *Object of Lust*. Another rush job, done to the background music of a wolf growling outside the door, but I think it's worthy of another shot at the gold ring."
—the Author from an interview with Ed Gorman

"Charles Runyon was a top notch writer who wrote masterpiece after masterpiece. Why he is not more well-known is a mystery."
—Dave Wilde

"Runyon's prose is very vivid, and all the characters are interesting."
—James Reasoner, *Rough Edges*

1

Once Lewis had seen her in a quilted bedjacket, once in a clinging white swimsuit. Today she wore black toreadors, white jersey, straw huaraches. He stopped her as she was about to drive off in her white Lincoln from the grocery store which served the lake's summer colony.

"Lewis!" she said, smiling through the rolled-down window. "I haven't seen you since the party."

"I've been working." Suddenly ill at ease, Lewis looked down and rubbed the shiny chrome of the window molding. He leaned against the car, feeling the hot smooth metal against his bare legs. He wore only red swimming trunks and sandals. "Just working, Marian," he said again.

Tiny wrinkles appeared around her mouth and betrayed the fact that she was straining to hold back a smile. "Teaching the high-school girls to water ski? Thrilling them with your daring feats, pyramids and jumps? Enjoying yourself?"

No, Marian, he thought. Don't make it light. You can't give me the light treatment after what happened three days ago.

"I've been trying to stay away from you," he said, looking at the polished chrome, "because of your husband." He raised his head and stared into her pale blue eyes. "It doesn't do a damn bit of good."

She turned away and chewed her lower lip. He inspected her greedily, liking the way her hair vaulted the spectrum from pale gold to burnt gold, whorled in back and fitting her scalp like a tight woven cap. He liked the feminine way in which her lip curved out, and the small, straight jaw.

"I'm going back to our lodge, Lewis," she said. "Would you like to drive a little way?"

He slipped in under the driver's seat and goosed the Lincoln down the winding asphalt road. Instead of turning into the drive leading to her lodge, he bounced the car along a dirt trail that followed the top of the ridge. She looked at him but said nothing. He felt a surge of hope and a hot, pulsing excitement. He stopped the car and stretched his arm along the back of the seat

"Come here," he said.

She slid into the crook of his arm and he kissed her. Her arms went around him and kneaded his back. Her mouth opened and her warm tongue moved between his lips.

After a minute he pulled away. "Come with me— somewhere, anywhere. Let's leave this place."

Her cheeks were spotted. Sweat dewed her upper lip. "Lewis, I'm afraid..."

Yes, he thought, you're afraid. You look at me and wonder if I have enough strength. Not only for myself, but for both of us.

"I know what you're afraid of," he said. "You're afraid it will be no good for me."

"You're twenty-two, and I'm thirty-five," she said.

"Don't," he said. "Don't talk like that. Let's get out."

The weeds were dusty along the side of the road, and dust sprayed his ankles as he led her through them. It was hot and still on the ridge. In the cove below, a fisherman's boat sat on the water like a silver bug trapped in glass.

He guided her to a place where the crab apple trees branched down to meet the tall clean grass. At one spot the grass was flattened as if someone had slept there.

She stopped. "You've been here before."

"Yes," he said. He didn't want to tell her that he had been here all morning, waiting for her to leave the lodge alone. He wasn't ashamed; *he* just wasn't ready to tell her. "Go on."

"Dee was sleeping when I left, but—"

"We can watch for your husband from here. Look." He pointed down to the square redwood lodge with the spidery steps descending to the beach below. "Go ahead."

She stopped to pass under the tree and snagged her hair. She did not move until he freed her. He had a weird feeling that she had suddenly decided to put herself in his hands; that if he told her to turn handsprings and eat grass, she would. He felt humble to think that she trusted him completely.

He sat down with his legs doubled under him. She lowered herself to one hip and rested her head against his chest. He kissed her and thought, *Nothing can keep me from her now.* He felt a cold urge to strip her and take her roughly, without any preliminaries, mashing her body into the hard ground as payment for the two days he had waited in torment.

But the end was certain, so he waited still. The heat rose in his body and he felt the tumescence of desire. He would have liked to hold the kiss, but his head was bent too low for comfort. He pulled away and lit a cigarette.

"Do you want to?" he asked.

"I'm afraid."

"You said that. Your husband?"

"No. I don't know."

"I do," he said. "You're afraid it wouldn't be any good the first time."

She looked startled. "Maybe it wouldn't. I've never tried to please a man."

"Sometimes when you do, you wind up pleasing

yourself the more." She looked puzzled, and he went on. "Look, it doesn't matter if it's no good the first time. It's like dancing. You have to learn your partner's manner, his way. You come to anticipate his movements. You..." He ran out of words and ended flatly, "I want it, but not if you don't. You have to tell me."

She leaned forward and kissed him. It was a funny kind of kiss, not demanding at all, only giving. It asked for no response, so he gave none.

After a moment she leaned back and began rubbing her palms over his bare chest. "You have a lovely chest, Lewis. Such nice pectoral muscles."

He wondered why she was being clinical. Maybe it helped her.

"Occupational stigma," he said. "Skiers get that way. When I sacked grain I got calloused fingertips. In the army I got a callous on the inside of my thumb from holding a carbine sling."

He had lost interest in what he was saying even before he had finished. Talk was postponement. He gripped her buttock and pulled her acquiescent body against him. There was a little hollow where her neck joined her shoulder. He pressed his lips into it.

"I'll mark you," he said. "How will you explain that to your husband?"

"You'd better not," she said. Her voice was strained and remote.

He slid the jersey and bra straps from her shoulders, baring the tops of her breasts. He did not bare the breasts completely because he thought she might be ashamed of them. She had a twelve-year-old-girl, and he felt that her breasts might not be perfect. But he loved them all the same. He touched his lips to the white flesh.

"I'll mark you there. Then you could never go back

to your husband."

"Lewis—don't talk about him."

He drew away from her, frowning. He knew why she didn't want to talk about her husband. She wanted to keep this incident separate; she wanted to shut it out of the rest of her life. The thought angered him. He stretched out his hand and jerked the jersey and bra down to her waist.

She gasped, but did not flinch.

"You want to go back?" he asked, looking at her. He saw that he had been wrong about her breasts. They were tight-fleshed and smooth, curving out and up like miniscule ski jumps to end in cones no darker than the tan on her shoulders. He saw the faint blue network of veins on their lower sides, and longed to hold their weight in his palms. He felt the blood pump strongly in his loins, almost painfully. *Now ... now ...* But still he waited, wanting her to make the decision.

"No," she said finally, "I don't want to go back."

"Sure?"

"Yes. But don't rush me, Lewis," she said in a gently scolding tone. "I'm not... skilled at this sort of thing."

"All right." He lay back and put his hands under his head, looking up at the sky. The crab apple leaves were brown at the edges. Needed rain. Birds twittered, and he heard a launch rumble out in the main lake. Marine inboard, he decided, about a hundred-thirty horsepower.

He heard the click of Marian's lighter, then smelled the smoke of her cigarette mingled with the faint bouquet of her perfume. He lay without moving, letting his strength curl and flow inside his body. Waiting would make it better. He knew that she would come to him. She owed it to him, just as she owed her life to him.

He closed his eyes and let his thoughts drift back to

that afternoon, three days ago. The lake had been rough. A strong southwest wind had swept the long axis of the lake and piled up waves four feet high. Nobody had any business skiing outside the sheltered coves, but the summer colony's drinking set hadn't known that ...

Lewis was piloting the Pla-Mo Resort's little training boat when the cruiser bounced past doing at least fifty. The woman on the end of the towline was having trouble. She had swung wide on the curve; now she was either too drunk or too unskilled to jump the wake and break her speed on the inner side of the curve. Her head jerked and her towline sagged and tightened as she bounced on the water. She went down and left her ski-belt floating on a patch of bubbles.

Lewis cut his engine, gulped air, and dived. The water was murky, shading downward into a lumpy darkness. He kicked deeper and saw that the dark lumps were drowned trees, still rooted to the soil. He felt his eyes bulge with the need for air, but he couldn't leave her down there. If she drifted into that twilight forest, he might lose her.

Then he saw her far to his right. He swam to her, grabbed a fistful of hair, and kicked himself toward the roof of light. His lungs swelled and pressed against his ribs ...

That night they invited him to a party on their terrace. Lewis disliked the bright, nervous gaiety. Talk of markets and real estate bored him. He sipped his drink and watched Marian. He remembered the firm wet feel of her legs as he had lifted her into his boat. He could still taste the coldness of her lips as he had breathed life into her lungs.

She relaxed on a chaise longue, wearing a quilted bedjacket. Sometimes she looked around with an odd, surprised expression, as though she had suddenly been transported to an unfamiliar place. The others treated her as an invalid; they brought her drinks and lit her cigarettes. They seemed to be playing a game, and Lewis grew annoyed.

When she was alone he walked over to her and put his hand on her shoulder. Her body seemed soft and pliable, relaxed. "Would you like to take a walk?"

She looked up at him, startled. "Oh, Leland. I'm fine right here."

"The name is Lewis," he said, increasing the pressure of his grip on her shoulder. "Come on. We have something to talk about."

She stiffened slightly under his hand, then went loose again. "Well, I really shouldn't leave the party, but..."

Just then a thin woman walked over, wearing a bare-midriff blouse and a flowing skirt. She had glittering eyes and thick black hair which hung to her shoulders like a gypsy's. Lewis had seen her around the lake, never twice with the same man. She wanted to refresh Marian's drink, but Lewis said she didn't need any more.

The woman raised hair-thin eyebrows. "Really?" She smiled down at Marian. "The young man now claims your life, Marian. It's an old Arab custom."

"Don't be silly, Carol." Marian took the drink and looked up at Lewis. "Dance with her, Lewis. I'd rather sit and watch."

Carol danced close, and her pelvic bone ground into his groin. "I saw you ski in the water carnival," she said. "You were magnificent."

He nodded, watching Marian. She was drinking too much; he wondered if she always did.

Carol leaned forward and spoke in his ear. "We're going next door to my place when this is over. Just a few of us, the lunatic fringe. I'd like you to come."

"Is Marian going?"

"No, she's the married type. But I'll see that you don't get lonely."

Lewis felt her lips on his neck, warm and wet. Her breath was heavy with liquor. She was drunk, she was easy; but she was not Marian. "No," he said.

She leaned back, using her pelvis as a fulcrum. "No, just like that?"

"I have to work tomorrow."

She smiled, as though working were a whim of his. "Don't you think you should find out what you're passing up?"

The record ended. Lewis dropped his arms and stepped away from her. "I'll ask around, Carol."

He turned and walked toward Marian. But Marian's husband stopped him. DeWitt was his name, but everybody called him Dee. He was a big man with red hair, but his bigness was not imposing. He was loosely built, as though someone had tacked on his joints with six-penny nails just to hold them in place while he went to get some screws. Dee was strong, though; his handshake popped the bones in Lewis' fingers, and for a moment Lewis liked the man.

He was a lawyer of some kind, and he told Lewis how grateful he was, speaking in the rounded overstatements lawyers affect when they're drinking. Lewis waited impatiently, wanting to go back to Marian.

Finally Dee trailed off, looking embarrassed. He fumbled for his billfold. "This is nothing ... I mean, no measure of my gratitude. But I want you to have it."

Lewis looked down at the hundred-dollar bill, then up at Dee. He had a feeling that he was being paid to go away.

"Keep it," he said. "I'm not interested in your money."

For a moment Dee just stared, eyes slowly turning hard while his smile remained fixed. It gave his face a grotesque, imbalanced look. Then the smile faded, too.

"You'd better go then. Because that's all you're going to get."

Lewis had walked to the edge of the terrace, then turned. Dee stood watching him with the money still in his hand; Marian was surrounded by friends. They'd shut him out, isolating him from Marian. Even the thin woman, Carol, was a part of the conspiracy.

He could not fight them all, so he went away. But he returned the next day, and the day after that. Now he had her beside him. He heard the rustle of dry grass as she put out her cigarette.

"Asleep, Lewis?" she asked.

"No," he said without opening his eyes.

There was a snapping, swishing sound, and he knew she was taking off bra and jersey. A moment later he sensed her presence above him; he felt her nipples brushing his chest like hard little fingertips. Then he felt the full weight of her breasts.

"I love you, Lewis," she said.

He opened his eyes and looked up at her. She has to have that, he thought. Love—not lust, not sex, not a woman's natural desire to fulfill herself with a man, no. Love. The social word, the woman's word. Probably she felt as he did, but it was the only word she knew to describe the fiery pounding of the blood, the lash of leaping desire. Well, by that definition...

"I love you too, Marian." His voice sounded tinny and flat. He fumbled with the zipper on the back of her slacks, but his fingers were like bananas.

"Why didn't you wear a dress?"

"They wrinkle."

He wondered how she knew that. Had she done this

before? He rose to his knees, feeling rough and brutal. "You do it."

She unzipped the toreadors and pushed them down to her hips, revealing white panties.

"Now let me," he said, feeling tender again. She raised her hips as he slid the clothes down. They caught on her heels and his hands were shaking by the time he got them off.

He raised his eyes and saw that she was watching him, looking down her body to where he squatted with her clothes in his hands. That body of hers was white from breast to thigh, gray-white and moist as though she had come out of a cocoon. Her stomach sank in like an ancient grave.

"You should tan that," he said. His throat hurt. He felt prickly and nervous; he didn't know why.

He looked at her and tried to read her emotions. Her eyes looked flat and wrinkled at the corners. Her face was mottled and her mouth tightly frozen. She is ready, he thought; if I wait any longer it will be no good for either of us.

Lewis heard a twig snap behind him. Marian's face turned the color of ashes; her lips parted and a tiny cry emerged.

Lewis turned slowly, half expecting to see her husband. Instead he saw two boys in their early teens. One held a butterfly net upraised; the other carried a screened box. They stood frozen, as though caught by a split-second shutter. They stared at the woman as though she were a strange animal, totally outside their experience. Lewis felt shunted aside, a spectator to this encounter between two boys and the woman he had exposed for their inspection.

The moment hung suspended for a dozen heartbeats, then Lewis found his voice.

"Beat it," he croaked.

Their eyes flicked over him, then returned to the woman. They didn't move.

"Get away from here!" He jumped to his feet.

The boys were off like two frightened antelopes. Lewis tore after them, suddenly realizing what it would mean if they talked about what they had seen. He wanted to catch them and cajole or bribe or beat them into silence.

But his height was a handicap. The low branches ripped his flesh and tore at his hair, while the boys scurried away. Finally he gave up and turned back. Sweat streamed down his body and mingled with the blood from his scratches.

He found Marian sitting up, fully dressed. She was looking down at her hands, twisting her wedding band with the slow, abstract motion of a person in shock.

"Did you catch them?" she asked as he sat down. Her voice sounded dull and flat, and he had a feeling she did not really care, but was asking just to kill the silence.

"No," he said. "But they won't be back."

"I've seen them before," she said in the same dead voice. "They—" Her voice caught. "They're my daughter's friends."

"Oh." He felt a shock of pity for her, and condemned himself for putting her in this position. Then he remembered that she had made the decision. He looked at her and saw the bits of leaves and grass clinging to her toreadors. He thought of how she looked without them and realized that he wanted her now more than ever. He also knew that the perfect moment had passed and would never come again, not even if they knew each other for fifty years.

I shouldn't have waited, he thought. I should never have left the initiative to her.

"You want a cigarette?" he asked.

"Oh, God. No! No! I've got to get out of here."

She rose slowly, like a convalescent who is just beginning to walk again. Lewis knew there was no point in asking her to stay.

"I'll get that foliage off you," he said, stretching out his hand.

"No. Don't touch me." She jerked away and looked at him with a mixture of horror and distaste. She looked at him as though he were a strange man who had come up behind her on the street and whispered something filthy in her ear.

Her lower lip quivered, then she whirled and ran out through the brush, ignoring the twigs which caught at her hair. A minute later he heard the whirring of her starter.

Lewis walked out on the ridge and watched the white Lincoln pull into the drive beside her lodge. Marian jumped out and ran to the door, then paused to look up at the ridge. Lewis could not read her expression at this distance, but he saw her shudder as if something cold had touched her flesh.

He watched for several minutes after she went inside. Then he turned and walked down the opposite slope to the cove where he had left his boat. He would have to start all over again the next time he found Marian alone.

He was certain of one thing. He could not let it end now.

2

At noon on the seventh day of watching, Lewis climbed the ridge for the fourteenth time, feeling a tight knot of anticipation in his stomach. What would she do today? What would she wear?

Yesterday she had worn white shorts and a red halter. She had raked their white crescent beach, sorting out the jagged chert and throwing it into the water. Sweat had glistened on her honey-colored back, and he had longed to touch his tongue to her flesh and taste the warm, salty moisture which came from inside her body.

My woman, he had thought. My woman.

Then her husband had come out with his rough voice and restless hands and spoiled everything. He hoped the man would be drunk today; drunk or dead.

He slid under the crab apple tree and set down his lunch beside him. His nest was littered with tiny wads of cigarette paper; he always field-stripped his butts and broke his matches. He did not want to start a fire.

He took his new binoculars from the case, surveying the cove as he did so. The fashionable summer homes spread out from the water's edge like iron filings disposed around a magnet. Nothing stirred. The lake was deep in its midweek lethargy.

He raised the binoculars and focused on her lodge. It lay in the sun like a dead grasshopper, an empty desiccated husk. He felt a stab of disappointment as he saw her husband's black Buick parked in the drive, and his inboard launch moored in its floating dock. The man was home.

Lewis saw Marian on the sun porch, lying face down on a lounge chair. Her black knit swimsuit was pushed down to her hips; dimples on each side of her spine marked the beginning swell of her buttocks. She turned her face toward him, away from the sun.

There were dark circles under her closed eyes and deeper lines around her mouth. She looked tired. They had gone to a party last night and Lewis had shivered on the ridge until two in the morning. When they had come home her husband and the bright-eyed woman, Carol, had to help her up the steps from the launch. Lewis wished she did not drink so much, but he understood ...

A boat whined into the cove and circled once, trailing a white carpet of wake. When it had gone, Marian raised herself to her elbows, looked around, then swung her feet to the deck of the sun porch. She picked up a towel and wiped the perspiration from the base of her neck and beneath her breasts. Lewis thought how white and defenseless she looked with her breasts exposed.

He felt no guilt about watching her. It was as though he had lived with her for seven days—and nights; all that time he had been waiting for her to come out alone. Her daughter was gone now, but Dee was always there, or the bright-eyed gypsy of a woman, Carol, who lived in a white lodge a hundred yards down the cove. And every night there had been parties.

Lewis had sent her a note on the second day, but she had not come to meet him. He had waited for her at the little store, but when she saw him she had driven away.

His food had begun to taste like sawdust; he had lost interest in his work and his ski practice. He tried to get a grip on himself but there was nothing to hold on to; the only real part of him was the part that desired Marian. Even his landlady had noticed.

"Don't think about it, whatever it is," she had told him. "That's what I do when something bothers me. I don't think about it." She had a mole with hair growing out of it and he hated her. She worked crossword puzzles and always did the horizontals before she ever touched a vertical.

Sure, he had wanted to say. Don't think about it. Erase it. You can erase it because your mind is flat, like a sheet of paper—all horizontals.

It would be nice, thought Lewis, to have a simple, controllable mind, instead of one through which black, warty thoughts flitted like bats through an attic.

He watched Marian pull up the swimsuit, bending forward and wriggling her shoulders as she confined her breasts. She lay down on her back and covered her eyes with the folded towel.

She would sleep now. In about fifteen minutes she would go in and take a shower, drying herself with painstaking care as though her body were a delicate vase for which she had paid a great price. She would smooth the invisible wrinkles around her eyes and pinch the flesh around her waist while her mouth made a *moue* of dissatisfaction.

It was a bad age for her; Lewis understood that. He understood her as well as her husband did, maybe better.

He knew she read magazines from back to front. He knew she got up before sunrise and drank an ounce or two of whiskey on the sun deck, looking out over the cove and not moving for minutes at a time. Three nights ago, Lewis knew, she had kissed a man who sold boats down at the dam. He was known locally as a lover of women, and Lewis hated him. Marian and the man had stood under the trees and smoked, then returned separately to the party. Later Lewis understood why Marian had done it. She was restless, searching, driven by the same gnawing hunger that had kept him sleepless for seven nights.

Lewis lowered his glasses and began eating the lunch his landlady had fixed. In ten minutes he had to get back to work; back to teaching the high-school girls who rubbed against him and giggled and asked him where he spent his nights. But he would be back to this ridge.

The time would come when he would spot her in that lodge alone. He would go down then. There would be no waiting for the right moment, no nonsense about getting her consent...

3

Dewitt Morgan woke up at one p.m. with gritty eyes and a pounding ache at the base of his skull. He kicked off the sheet and lit a cigarette. He smoked without taking the cigarette from his mouth, his big hands clasped on his naked chest. Uneasily, he let his mind drift over the previous evening.

Marian, drunk again. Carol with a wild gleam in her eyes which fit his own mood. They had put Marian to bed and gone on drinking. Toward morning they had made love, in a sudden, soundless blaze of passion, like two animals alone in the woods. "You're rough," she had said later, and he had felt omniscient and smoothly powerful, like Zeus.

Funny, he told himself now, I don't feel guilty. I thought a husband was supposed to feel guilty when he cheated.

But he knew that guilt did not come suddenly, like the falling of a curtain after a play. Now his emotions were exhausted; he was a cat lying before the fire, replete. When his nerves woke up the remorse would come. He would think of his daughter and of Marian, and he would resolve never to cheat again. But remorse would pass; he would do it again, and his marriage would go on unraveling, like a torn shirt flapping in the wind ...

He rolled out of bed and jerked on his Bermuda shorts. He found Marian on the sun porch, looking tired and drawn in the white sunlight.

She squinted up at him, then touched her fingers to her hair. "Well... it certainly is nice to see you up so early."

He decided to ignore her sarcasm. "Are we going to eat?"

She sat up and shrugged. "Go ahead. There are eggs and stuff in the refrigerator." She lifted a glass from beneath the chair and sipped a white murky liquid. "I'm having mine."

"Lemonade?"

"A squirt of lemon. Egg white." She smiled. "Mostly gin."

Dee felt a helpless frustration. He could not reach her any more. She was fire and ashes; hysteria and listlessness. And she drank too much.

"Where did you go last night?"

She shrugged. "Home, I guess. I woke up here."

Dee felt a quarrel building, and he could not stop it. He was like a man who stands on a river bank and feels himself sliding helplessly toward the water.

"You left the party for two hours," he said. "Where did you go?"

Her chin came up. "Where do you think I went?"

He leaned back against the hot boards of the cabin, trying to be calm and judicial, the way a lawyer should be. "Marian, I know what it means around here when a woman disappears from a party."

Her lips tightened. "You think I went with a man?"

Dee was sorry he had brought it up. He did not believe she was having an affair; at least, it had not reached the climax. He would know when it did, just as he had known years ago when she spent the car payment for a new dress. He dreaded the moment, but he realized there were few husbands who did not have to face it, sooner or later. He had always felt it looming up in his future like a rugged mountain he would some day have to scale.

There was another mountain, too. Sooner or later Marian would become aware that she was no longer beautiful to all men, would see a man's eyes slide over her and settle on a younger woman. Dee had always wanted to foresee these crises far enough in advance to protect her from them. But something was happening to bring them on earlier than he had expected.

A week ago she had come home from the store with her hair tangled, with grass stains and leaves on her clothing. She had been taut and quivering. When he had tried to learn what had happened, she had twisted his words into an accusation. The next day she had rushed Sharon off to camp. Dee had wondered about that, too, but he had not pushed it. The whole situation was like a letter which contained bad news. He was afraid to open it....

His mind leaped to what had happened two days later. "Have you received any more notes from him?"

Her face stiffened. "Whom?"

"The young man who saved you."

"Oh." She lowered her eyes and raised her glass. "No. Just the one."

"You haven't seen him?"

"No!" She looked at him, her eyes blazing. "Dee, give me credit for some discretion. He's only a boy."

Only a boy, thought Dee. He could not forget the note's matter-of-fact directions for her to meet him at the dam. No preliminaries; just instructions. Dee felt that something must have passed between them earlier; the young man must have had some basis for assuming Marian would meet him.

But here again, he was treading on dangerous ground ...

"Boys get ideas they aren't mature enough to

handle," he said, trying to ease away from the subject. "Their glands control them."

She rose to her feet, her mouth tight. "Keep an eye on your own glands, counselor, I'm going to take a shower."

Dee watched her walk inside, peeling down her swimsuit. Her remark about glands made him wonder if she knew about him and Carol, then he decided she had been too drunk to notice anything.

He went into the kitchen, got a picnic ham from the icebox, and started making a sandwich. He wondered if Carol would draw any conclusions about last night. Surely not. She knew better than anyone else that he had never really been interested in any woman but Marian. Carol had been in on it from the beginning; in fact, he had been dating Carol when he had met Marian, her roommate ...

They had formed an odd contrast—Carol, thin and feverishly passionate, and Marian, cool and strangely passive, besides being the most beautiful girl he had ever seen. They had gone to one of those basement parties—in a frat house rathskeller—where all the lights are turned out at ten.

Marian's date, a football player, had gotten sloppy and Dee, finding her alone, had said: "You aren't having any fun."

"I might have," Marian had said, "if I'd stick closer to you." And somehow the evening had ended with Dee kissing Marian good night in the front seat while Carol wrestled with the football player in the back.

The last fifteen years had been an extension of that night; Dee and Marian together, while Carol ran through the football player, an engineering student, a nightclub manager, then two husbands and so many other men that Dee had lost count.

But she had never been far from his fingertips, and

Dee had always felt that he had only to stretch out his hand and Carol would be there. The fact that he had gone fifteen years without reaching did not give Dee a warm glow of self-satisfaction. No, an available woman tempted him as much as the next man; but he had always been able to say to himself: *I've got something better waiting for me at home.* Until last night ...

But last night had not been important. Carol had been a means of cooling his body—something like a cold shower. She posed no threat to his marriage, so Dee decided not to worry about her.

The boy was different. Dee had thought about him several times during the last ten days. What was his name? Yes, Lewis. Dee thought of the party, when he had been so happy to have Marian alive that he would have done anything for Lewis.

But the boy had been oddly repellent. There was something unnaturally clean and stark about his good looks. His face was composed of straight planes which met in perfect angles. You couldn't say about him: here is a thoughtful young man, or a happy one, or a sad one, or a vicious one. His face was neutral. His silence was not a thoughtful silence, but something deeper than that. He seemed non-human, a machine.

Dee had seen him watching Marian, and had felt a chill of fear for her. He had wanted Lewis to leave, so he had offered him money ...

Dee remembered another face. The face of a sixteen-year-old boy who had shot his father after being forbidden the use of the family car. Dee had then been a prosecuting attorney, and he had tangled with the legal question of sanity. Did the boy know right from wrong? Yes, said the boy, he knew. He wanted the car. His dad wouldn't let him have it. That was wrong. Was it wrong to shoot his father?

"I don't know," the boy had said. "Yes, I guess so," he had added with a silly grin. "They put me in jail for it."

The case had sickened Dee. And now Lewis reminded him of that boy. Lewis was the same kind, Dee thought; the kind that might know right from wrong but would never let such knowledge interfere with his desires. Lewis was not as far gone as the other boy, but traveling the same road. He wasn't stupid. He wasn't warped. But there was something missing. You talked to him and you felt the way you do when you climb dark stairs and expect another step. Your foot comes down hard and a quick nausea stabs you in the guts. Something should be there and isn't ...

Dee picked up the sandwich and started to bite into it. Suddenly he stopped and stared at the calendar above the stove. August fourteenth. He had to be in court tomorrow. The Tasty Dip outfit was fighting an injunction from the dairy association, which was trying to keep Tasty Dip from using the word "cream" in its advertising. He was to meet their attorneys at five this evening.

He did not want to leave Marian in her present mental state.

Well, he wouldn't. He went into the bathroom and spoke over the shower curtain, asking her to go back to the city with him. "No need to open the house," he said. "We'll stay in a hotel and come back tomorrow evening."

She slid back the curtain and stepped to the mat. "It would bore me."

He watched as she propped a smooth leg on the stool and began probing between her toes with the towel. Her shoe straps had left streaks of white on her tanned feet. He saw that the flesh had begun to ripple on the insides of her thighs. She's thirty-five, he remembered with a shock. And I'm almost forty.

"Maybe we should get away together," he said gently.

"We're away together right here. I can't see that it's done any good."

He felt a stirring of anger, but he couldn't stop it. "You'll sit here and drink yourself into a stupor, or else ..."

She looked up. "Or else what?"

"Or you'll see that man, whoever he is."

Her jaw set. "Thanks for the suggestion."

She walked into her bedroom and slammed the door. After a minute he followed her and knocked. She did not answer. He doubled his fists and started to pound on the door. Then he turned away. The quarrel would grow and grow until it went out of control. Best to end it. She wasn't herself.

He went into his own bedroom and began to pack an overnight bag. What had happened to the good old days? Once they had shared something close to perfection; no quarrels, no boredom, no jealousy, not even irritation. Take the first time they had made love ...

It was the Saturday before the homecoming game; the sound of hammers had echoed across from Greektown, where the frat rats were putting up their displays. It was his last year, and the kind of day that joins students into pairs and drives them into the woods. A warm sun, with the wind brushing against you like a cool woolly blanket.

He walked her into a glen of maples and asked her to marry him. She wore a plaid skirt, a white blouse and a button-type sweater, and those black and white saddle shoes which were popular then. She was silent for a long time, stirring up leaves with the edge of her shoe.

He noticed how the fold of her sock made her ankle

seem thicker than it was, but accented the sudden taper of her calf. Desire swelled in his chest and nearly choked him. She was silent so long that he was afraid she would refuse him, so he started talking fast, describing his plans and how much money he would make.

She looked at him with her eyes bright and said, "You think I care about that? I love you."

For a while they talked in senseless phrases, then they made love on the maple leaves with the sound of hammers in the distance. It was her first time, and that was like a bonus because Dee had not expected it. Later he picked the leaves from her skirt and felt hungry. They walked uptown and ate pizza, rolling it into cylinders so the juice ran out into his hand and streamed down the lifeline of his palm. Cheese and green pepper, with the crust thin and crisp against his teeth.

For several years, eating pizza had been an anniversary rite. Then by mutual consent it had been halted. They weren't making pizza like they used to; they weren't making love like they used to ...

He jerked shut the zipper of the overnight bag. He put on his suit, feeling the cloth tingle against his legs. He had grown unaccustomed to clothing these last two weeks.

He carried his bag to the car and slid in behind the front seat. He opened the glove compartment and took out his .38 revolver. It had a heavy frame and a springclip shoulder holster. He had acquired it when he was a prosecuting attorney, in the days when every other man he put away was threatening to get him.

He loaded the cylinder, set the safety, then went inside and knocked on Marian's door.

"It's a three-hour drive, so I'm going now," he said. "I want to give you something."

She opened the door, and he saw that her nose was bright red on the tip. She had been crying. She never used to cry; the last ten days had seemed to peel away her armor, leaving the raw pink flesh of her emotions exposed to the world.

Exposed, too, was a foot-wide expanse of nakedness, left bare by the robe draped over her shoulders. She was still the most beautiful woman he had ever seen. He wanted to make love to her, to burn away the wisps of their quarrel which lingered in the air like the smell of yesterday's boiled cabbage. But there wasn't time; Marian was one woman you didn't get into bed by snapping your fingers, not even if you happened to be her husband ...

He took the gun from his pocket. "Keep this handy while I'm gone."

She looked at him, surprised. "Why?"

He was thinking of Lewis, but he said, "Prowlers. They may come around."

She looked at the gun as though it were a dead mouse. "No. I couldn't use it. I couldn't."

"I'd feel better if you had it."

"Well, leave it then. But I won't use it."

"All right. Goodbye."

She turned her cheek to him and he kissed her. Then he left the gun on the bar and walked to his car. As he started to get in, he felt the hair prickle on the back of his neck. A cold draft seemed to have swept down from the top of the ridge. He looked up, but the air was still as death; the crab apple leaves hung like lead weights.

He got in the car and drove off, but he couldn't shake his uneasiness. When he reached the city, he would call Carol. He would ask her to look after Marian.

4

Marian felt lonely when she heard her husband drive off. She put on shorts and a halter and walked to the bar in the living room. She touched her fingers to the gun and thought of the bullets bulging out of their cases like little lead eyes.

She shivered, then she pushed out the cylinder, the way Dee had once shown her, and removed the cartridges. She put the gun on one shelf, below the bar, and the cartridges on another. She didn't want things too easy. She was afraid she might get an impulse to grab the gun and send one of those little lead eyes searching through her own brain.

She started looking over the bottles. They had stocked a lot of junk when they had moved in; the usual Scotch, bourbon and gin, along with vodka, rum, metaxa, tequila. Most of the bottles were empty

She felt a stab of guilt. I drank practically all of that, she thought. How long had it taken? She didn't know. Days were numbers, all alike and meaningless except as a quantity. Time had gone out of her life ...

There was some tequila left. She poured out a glassful and savored its acrid metallic odor. How did you drink it? Yes, a wedge of lemon, and a pinch of salt between thumb and forefinger. Switch-itch, somebody called it. Too much trouble.

She took it straight, feeling it slide past her tongue and down her throat with no more sensation than a drink of water would have evoked. She felt a gentle explosion in her stomach, though; felt the heat flow out in all directions. A return wave reached her tongue and she tasted the hot-cold biting, like dry ice.

Oh, that's good. *Goood.* She drank another, then

picked up the letter she had received from her daughter and carried it, together with the bottle and glass, out to the sun deck that overlooked the cove.

In the letter, Sharon said her camp was all right, but she missed the crowd at the lake. She had reached the age at which boys were something more than playmates who went to different bathrooms, so most of her questions concerned boys she knew, among them the two who had seen Marian on the ridge.

Thank God, thought Marian, I got her away before she found out. Thank God for that reprieve, however short it may be.

Sharon had sent a picture of herself dressed in the camp uniform. She had Dee's red hair and his heavyboned features; she had also inherited his proclivity to freckle instead of tan. Too bad, thought Marian, that Sharon had not fared better in the distribution of genes. She should have had Marian's complexion and Dee's steady encompassing mind; instead, these things were reversed in the child.

Marion tried to answer the letter, but her thoughts kept melting away like snow in the sun. She dropped the writing pad in her lap and looked out over the cove. The afternoon lay like a weight on her back. A wave rolled in from the main lake and splashed down the shore of the cove. It sounded like youngsters running through shallow water.

It's a lie, she thought. You're supposed to savor life after you nearly die. But you don't. Instead, you count up the score. You realize life is a temporary affair, and you add up what you've had from it. You've grown up under strict parents, you've gone to school and behaved properly, you've gotten married and you've had a daughter. Now you wonder. Is this it? Is this all there is?

Once she had taken comfort in being able to predict

the rest of her days. In a few years Dee would take on a younger partner. Then, when he felt the tide running again for his party, he would go back into politics; perhaps he would become attorney general.... And so on into the pale rose twilight, while his faithful wife grew old at his side, an extension of the man and no more...

Lately she had been resenting her symbiotic state. She had made love to only one man in her entire life, and she wondered if that were not the problem. She had decided to change matters, so that if she did not come up the next time, she could say to herself: well, at least I've had this much—a sex adventure.

Lewis had looked clean and handsome in his swimsuit and sandals that morning. *This is the one,* she had thought. *I can do it with him.* She owed him something, true; but that was only an excuse she had made to herself. She would have tried to seduce him anyway.

But Lewis was like a stove that gives off flashes of heat but no warmth. He made her edgy and nervous. She had thought it was a part of being her first time and she had tried to ignore it, just as she had tried to ignore his strange, shifting personality. After that horrible moment of discovery by those children, she had known she had made a mistake. There was something wrong about Lewis. She had fled from him, hoping she would never see him again, thinking that at least the incident had cured her unrest.

But three nights ago she had met Joe Forrest, a man of thirty-five or so, who boasted a small mustache and the biggest boat business on the lake. She had been bored with the party, and Joe's attention had stimulated her—so she had hesitated only a moment when he had suggested they take a walk.

"I can't stand these damn social charades for very

long, Marian," he had said when they were out under the trees. "The wives talk about this, the husbands talk about that, and the whole damn thing is as boring and unspontaneous as a political convention. The only reason a man comes is to get next to the other man's wife. It's like a checker game—you work to get into the other man's king row and at the same time keep him out of yours."

"Then you don't play fair, Joe," she said. "You don't have a wife to risk."

He laughed. "That's why I'm a safe companion. There's no Mrs. X, no unknown factor to blow up into a nasty affair."

Marian had gone back inside after a single kiss, because she had known him less than an hour and her experience with Lewis had made her cautious. But his thinly veiled promise had intrigued her; here was a man skilled enough to get her over the rough spots so gently she wouldn't even feel them.

Last night she had gotten drunk enough to put her conscience to sleep, and had gone out with Joe in his cabin cruiser. She had let him handle her in the dark cabin and had waited for the stir of desire. It had been slow in coming; slower than it had ever been with Dee. When Joe had begun to undress her, the cool leather of the seat had shocked her bare flesh. Her body had gone stiff and cold. She had seized Joe's wrists and halted his searching hands.

"What's wrong?" he had asked.

"It's no good, Joe," she said. "I guess I'm just a one-man woman."

Joe had sat up, had lit a cigarette for each of them. "There's no such animal, kid. You're scared of something."

She knew it was a reaction to the affair with Lewis, but she said, "Maybe I'm scared that I'd hate myself afterward."

Joe was silent a minute, then nodded. "No doubt. But hating yourself is part of doing what you want to do. You choose between frustration and guilt, because you're going to feel one or the other no matter what you do."

He's clever with women, she had thought. He falls into my mood and tries to lead me out of it without letting me know I'm being manipulated.

But Dee had always done the same thing, so it had not worked for Joe. Instead, she had thought of Dee, waiting at the party.

"Let's get back, Joe."

She had put on the blouse he had removed, and had fastened her stockings. Her cocktail skirt had gotten bunched under her, so she turned it and tried to smooth out those horizontal wrinkles which Carol said betrayed so many women. Then she saw that Joe had not moved.

"Joe, it's getting late. You'd better take me back."

"I'm not sure I'll take you back."

She had felt a quiver of fear. "What?"

"Suppose I just slammed you down on the seat and took what I wanted? You wouldn't yell. You want to be forced into it, so you won't have to blame yourself."

Marian had realized then he wasn't serious.

"Come on, Joe. Dee will get suspicious and make a scene."

He flipped his cigarette into the water and walked to the wheel. "I'm doing this because you want me to, not because I'm afraid of that overgrown husband of yours. But I warn you, one of these days you'll run into someone who'll do just what I said. You're too damn pretty a woman to play this teasing game. An ugly broad could get away with it; a guy decides after a while that she's not worth the time and trouble. But you ... a man gets permanent ideas about a woman like you. He doesn't mind spending some time as long as he sees a chance; he might not even mind risking a rape charge."

Marian had thought about that on her way back to the party. She remembered Lewis, the note he had written and the way he had waited for her at the store. Thank God, he seemed to have given up ...

Joe had stopped her as she had started to get out of the boat. "One more thing, Marian. I like to think I've got self-control, but I can't go through another deal like this. When you're sure you're ready, you call me. Okay?"

"I never called a man in my life, Joe. Goodbye."

She had gone back to the party feeling disappointed in herself. She had gotten drunk, but it had not helped.

Now she looked into her glass and thought, with a feeling of abandon that had no joy in it—Well, here I go again ... She reached for the tequila and found that she had emptied the bottle. She carried it inside and dropped it into the garbage can. A half-dozen cockroaches scurried out.

Two weeks before, the sight would have sent her into a paroxysm of cleaning; now it did not seem important. But it was an alternative to drinking, so she got the roach powder and started dusting.

Later Carol came over for coffee. She looked as though she needed it. Her dark, nocturnal beauty had never worn well in the daytime. Now her hands were shaky, her eyes puffy. She wore shorts and halter, and you could see her ribs, her thin legs and the patches of blue color where she shaved her armpits.

Marian liked being around Carol, partly because Carol made her look good. And Carol stayed around Marian—or so Marian suspected—because that's where Dee usually was. It was an odd framework for friendship, but it had endured fifteen years. Dee had sold Carol's second husband a piece of their lake frontage. In the divorce settlement, which Dee had handled, Carol had taken the lake house. Now she lived there alone.

Today Carol was blaming herself for the failure of her marriages. Her fluffy black hair hung down over her eyes, and she held her cigarette between stiff fingers while she clutched a cup of coffee in her other hand.

Marian decided Carol must have misbehaved the night before. Marian had sat through enough of Carol's morning-after confessionals to recognize one in the making. It was like old times in the campus coffee shop; Carol in the throes of *Weltschmerz,* quoting Omar Khayyam and staring into her cup as though she wished it were a bottomless pit and she were in it...

".... The worst part of divorce," Carol was saying, "is the way it chops your life into little pieces. I remember with Harry I'd occasionally slip up and mention Mike. There'd be trouble ... not much trouble, but enough to make me gradually stop talking about the years with Mike. Then I stopped thinking about them. They were just gone. My life became like a film with a piece edited out ..." Carol sighed. "They were both good men. Maybe I don't want a good man. Maybe I want one as bad as I am." She looked at Marian. "Dee's a good man."

"Yes," Marian agreed, wondering if Dee and Carol had ever made love. She thought not; but only because Dee had never appeared interested. She did not think Carol would have hesitated; for her, liking a man and going to bed with him were almost synonymous.

"Marian, what's happened to the kid?"

"Kid? You mean Sharon?"

"The aquacade Adonis. The one who fished you up."

"I don't know," Marian said. "I don't care."

"He hasn't been around?"

"No, he hasn't been around." Marian felt uncomfortable. "Look, does it matter?"

"No ... I just thought if he showed up—"

"He won't."

"But if he comes around making trouble while Dee's gone, just point him in my direction. Okay?"

Marian frowned at Carol. What the hell made her think Lewis would make trouble. Or that she could handle it better than she, Marian. No, the whole thing sounded like one of Dee's plots. He and Carol were always forming alliances to protect his poor wife from some imaginary evil.

Marian was sure of one thing: she didn't want Lewis to talk to Carol, or Dee, or anyone else she knew. She didn't want anyone to learn what had happened on the ridge.

"All right Carol. If he shows up, he's yours. Now let's talk about something else."

Toward sunset they decided to barbecue hamburgers on the terrace. Marian changed to her yard-mowing jeans and a long-sleeved flannel shirt. The trees seemed to draw cold air like magnets. Darkness seeped in slowly, then a red convertible stopped in the drive.

It was one of Carol's friends. He wanted to take her for a drive. Carol said no, but Marian could see that she wanted to go. Marian was annoyed that Dee should think she needed a keeper, and she insisted that Carol go.

"Okay, but I'll be back early. If anything happens—"

"I'll scream," said Marian. "Now go."

After she left, Marian felt a stab of loneliness. The night was black outside the perimeter of the porch light. The wind had risen. It moaned through the narrow gap which divided the cove from the main lake, pushing crescent wrinkles into the gray water.

And then she was not alone.

"You've got too much fire," said a voice.

She whirled to see Lewis stride into the light, his tread silenced by crepe-soled sandals. He wore slacks with a crease like the blade of an axe. Threads of gold glinted in his black knit shirt.

He stopped and gave her a blue-steel look. "You remember me?"

Marian thought of a weird twilight forest in the cold deep water. She thought of death; of leaden limbs and a spreading coldness in her lungs. Then she remembered two pairs of wide adolescent eyes staring at her naked body.

"Lewis ... Please go away."

"I'm glad you remember my name." He smiled, then bent down to the barbecue pit. "You're burning your burgers. I could smell them a mile away."

She watched him rake out the charcoal and wondered how Dee would have advised her to get rid of him. Once at a convention she had slapped a man who tried to kiss her in the hall. Dee had been angry. You must have done something, he said, because a man doesn't try to move in on a woman unless he's got some reason to believe she'll let him. If you can't discourage a man without slapping him, you've lost the battle. And there are too damn many men who only get more excited when they're slapped.

Marian had a feeling Lewis was the latter type. Either that or something completely alien to Dee's world of men.

"Lewis," she said, "I'm asking you nicely to leave. You shouldn't be here."

He stood up and looked at her, leaning his head to one side. She noticed that his pale blue eyes never blinked.

"Your husband isn't home," he said.

"He'll be right back."

Lewis pulled a leaf from a low-hanging branch and ran his thumb over it, smiling as though the action were deeply satisfying. Marian heard a distant rumble of thunder.

"Your husband left with an overnight bag," said Lewis softly.

She felt as though something cold and slimy had crawled up her back. He's been watching the house, she thought, and shivered. She saw that somehow, without her being aware of it, he had gotten between her and the house.

"My girl friend will be back," she said.

"When?"

"Soon. Any minute."

He stood rubbing the leaf and smiling. "It wouldn't take long ... to finish what we started a week ago."

Suddenly she remembered Carol's house, not more than fifty yards behind her. She whirled and ran toward it as fast as she could, her jeans flapping against her ankles. The move must have taken Lewis by surprise, because she made it inside and was latching the screen door when his crepe soles pounded across the porch.

He grabbed the door and shook it, then dropped his hands. "You're just making it worse, Marian," he said in a tone of regret. "It's going to happen sooner or later."

"Lewis, if you aren't gone in one minute I'll call the sheriff."

"Call him."

She slammed the door and locked it. Then she ran around through the house and locked all the windows. By the time she finished the rain had arrived and was trying to tear the roof off the house.

She flipped on the porch light and peered through a window. Lewis was leaning against the porch railing. The rain had pounded his hair flat on his head and was running in a stream from his straight nose. He had turned his face toward the slanting drops and wore a satisfied expression, as though the rain were his own private possession.

Then he turned, looked at her, forced a grin. A stiff, lop-sided grin that made him look as though he were wearing a rubber mask.

She felt nausea tug at her stomach. *God, he's insane. That's why he always made me feel creepy. He's a psycho.*

She ran to the phone and lifted the receiver. The sheriff? Of course she couldn't call the sheriff. That would bring the whole affair out in the open.

She found Joe's number in the book and dialed it.

"Joe, this is Marian."

"Yes?" His tone was polite, but not warm.

She hesitated, feeling the weakness in her knees and the damp prickle of sweat inside her flannel shirt. She could hear music and the sound of laughter at the other end. She felt an aching need for the company of normal people.

"Joe, are you busy?"

"I have a few friends here. Why?"

"Could you send them away?"

"Maybe. Why should I?"

Oh, damn you, Joe. You're going to make me ask for it. I've never had to ask a man for anything in my life.

"I... I want to come over."

He paused, then said, "All right, I'll ease them off. Sit tight and I'll come and get you."

"Joe, wait—"

"Yes?"

She'd planned to tell him she just wanted company; not the thing they'd almost done last night. But she knew that if she said that, he wouldn't come.

"I'll be in the white cottage next door, Joe. But hurry. I'm ... ready now."

She hung up and looked through the window again. She couldn't see Lewis out there anywhere, but she had a feeling he wasn't far away.

She went to Carol's liquor cabinet and poured a drink from the first bottle she came to. It happened to be metaxa. The fiery Greek brandy seared her throat on the way down, but it was just what she needed. She drank another, then took the bottle and a glass to the kitchen table and sat down to get ready for Joe.

5

Carol saw Joe's Lincoln leave the graveled drive just as she and her date turned into it. She caught only a glimpse of the car, then Joe was gone with a squeal of tires on the asphalt road which led around the cove. Joe was in a hell of a hurry, she thought, and only one thing could make Joe hurry. He had a warm one in his car, and wanted to get her to his cabin before she cooled off.

Marian, of course. Who else?

Carol waited until George stopped beside her house, then she put her hand on his arm. "Georgie, do you mind? There's no point to coming in."

"Well, hell! Ten minutes ago you wanted to hurry and get back to the house."

"It came on suddenly, Georgie. Don't be angry. We'll make it some other time, huh?" She leaned over for a kiss, but he turned his face away and her lips brushed his check. "Good night," she said, and got out of the car. George left, spurting gravel all the way up her drive. Poor kid, didn't get his candy tonight. Just like the rest of the bastards, she thought without anger; they only want one part of me, and when they can't get that they want nothing.

She slipped into her own car and followed the asphalt road around the lake, then turned down the rutted gravel lane leading to Joe's secluded cabin. Few of the men knew it existed, and few of the women didn't. They regarded it as an assignation place, and therefore holy in its way, and even the women who never came here kept Joe's secret from their husbands—just in case they changed their minds. Carol had spent perhaps a half-dozen nights in the cabin, but they had meant little to either her or Joe. They had both happened to have time on their hands ...

She stopped her car two hundred yards from the cabin so that the sound would not alarm the two. She took off her shoes and walked gingerly, stifling the gasps which rose to her lips when gravel cut into her bare feet. A few feet from the house, Carol squatted on her haunches and peered through a lighted window. Through the lattice of a Venetian blind she saw Marian seated alone on the couch with a drink in her hand. Her eyes were wild, her cheeks flushed with alcohol. A moment later Joe appeared from his bedroom, wearing a purple bathrobe and carrying something black and sheer. He held it out and spoke. Carol, who knew Joe's routine, could almost hear him saying:

"Here. You might as well make yourself comfortable."

Marian took a long drink, stood up, staggered slightly, then accepted the negligee and left the room. Joe opened a fresh pack of cigarettes, dumped them into a wooden cigarette box and set it on the coffee table. Beside that he placed a bottle and a bucket of ice. He turned out all the lights except a dim, blue-shaded lamp beside the couch. He flicked a wall switch, and muted stereophonic music wafted from a hidden speaker at each end of the room. Then he sat back and sipped his drink with a calm and confident look on his face.

Carol, looking into that room of gleaming brass and polished wood, felt a prickle of envy. The thick white rug on the floor made her remember its soft, sensuous caress on her naked back. Joe was an artist: when your teeth grated with frustration, when you hated men and hated yourself because you needed them, he carried you into this little love-nest and made you his queen. It was more than love-making; he gave you affection, respect and a feeling that the simple biological act of mating was a noble, glorious achievement. Next morning you got breakfast in bed and quiet conversation, with no emotional hangover. You were two friends who had gotten together for mutual enjoyment. The project had been successful; you owed him nothing, and he owed you nothing ...

Yes, Carol envied Marian; she always seemed to get men without trying, ever since she'd stolen Dee that night in the rathskeller of the fraternity house. Oh, damn her...

Marian appeared, walking carefully with her drink held in front of her. Joe stood up and said something which Carol knew was a comment on Marian's beauty. Carol had to admit it was not idle flattery. Marian had brushed her hair until its golden highlights gleamed. Her body was a soft, rounded whiteness beneath the sheer black negligee; her tilted breasts strained upward, pulling the fabric away from the white expanse of her flat stomach.

Yes, thought Carol, if I were a man I would want

Marian myself. Or if I were a certain kind of woman ...

The pair sat and drank, and nothing happened for several minutes. Carol's muscles cramped, but she dared not move. Joe stroked Marian's hair and talked. Marian nodded abstractedly from time to time, and twice held out her glass to be refilled. Carol was puzzled. For a woman who had come so willingly and stripped so readily, Marian seemed remarkably cool. Joe parted the curtain of the gown, bared one pink-nippled breast, and bent down. Marian looked over his head, her face blank and almost indifferent. Carol hated her then; even outside, with the gravel cutting into her feet, she, Carol, could feel the heat of Joe's caress. After a moment Joe rose and spoke to Marian. She nodded matter-of-factly, as though consenting to a second cup of coffee. Joe stretched out his hand to the little lamp, Marian stood up and shook the gown off her shoulders, and then the room went dark—

Carol rose carefully, walked stiffly and cautiously to her car. The scene had left her skin hot, and she could feel the warm juices flowing inside her. She concentrated on turning the car around, then negotiating the gravel track. Now what, she wondered, as she turned onto the asphalt. By now little Marian has had it; sweet innocent Marian is lying flat on her satin-soft back on a couch which has held the thumping weight of half the women in the lake's summer crowd. Dee had asked her to take care of Marian, but she was already being taken care of, so ...

Once on the highway, Carol aimed the car toward the city. This is it, girl, she told herself; the moment you've been sweating out for fifteen years. Now you've got it right in the palm of your hand; a little wedge of evidence you can use to make the gap between them wider and wider, until at last you split them completely apart and make a place for yourself.

As she drove, holding the speedometer at a dangerous level, she began to wonder: What shall I tell him? Shall I report exactly what I saw? The hell of it is when you pass on a story like that, part of the blame always falls on you, because you were the informer. In the old days they used to chop off the head of a courier who brought bad news. It would serve no purpose to break them up if Dee comes to hate me—

By the time she reached Dee's hotel, she had decided to approach him slowly, then back out if it looked sticky.

She knocked on the door, feeling a tingle of anticipation at the prospect of seeing Dee. He opened the door in his pajamas, looked at her sleepily, then paled. "Carol! Has something happened to Marian?"

"She's all right," Carol said quickly. "I ... wanted to see you."

"Oh, for Christ's sake! And you left her there alone?" He started back into the room, then turned and said impatiently, "Well, come in. Come in. Don't just stand there."

She walked in, wishing she had not come. She sat down on the bed with her purse in her lap and felt like a fool. She watched Dee hurriedly lift the telephone, heard him give the number of his cabin.

"What? Lines down! For how long?" He paused to listen, then said: "Well. Call me as soon as you can get through. It's an emergency."

He hung up and looked at Carol, his face lined with worry. "The storm blew down a tree across the line. They're working on it now."

He ran bony fingers through his tangled red hair and sighed. Carol felt an urge to go over and smooth it down for him, press her lips to his; she was bursting to tell him not to worry about Marian because she was at this moment in bed with another man. But she sat still, painfully aware that he was angry at her for leaving Marian alone.

"I'm sorry, Dee. I guess I shouldn't have left her."

"Forget it." He stood up abruptly. "I need a drink. You?"

"I could stand one."

He poured two water glasses half-full of bourbon, then added ice water. Watching him, she thought: damn, it happened last night after so many years, and we are no more to each other than we were before. Too drunk; too drunk for it to have any importance, too drunk for it to have any after-effect, just a vague memory of passion and pleasure.

And she thought, I want him again, tonight. Let him find out about Marian in his own way; I won't tell him because he would become angry and bitter and that would cool it for me.

She took the glass he handed her and said: "You want me to go back?"

He shrugged and sat down on the bed. "Suit yourself."

"I'd rather stay here. With you."

He gave her a quick glance of annoyance, then sighed and began explaining patiently, as though to a child. "Carol ... last night was a result of liquor, nothing else. I don't want you to think it's the start of an affair. I shouldn't have done it, and I won't do it again."

"You didn't like it?"

He eyed her curiously. "Is that important?"

"Yes. To me."

He looked at his glass and spoke thoughtfully: "I'll tell you the truth, since it won't happen again. Yes, I liked it. You were ... unrestrained. There was no reluctance, and I had a feeling you were enjoying it as much as I. It wasn't like ..."

"Like Marian?" Immediately she wanted to take back the words. His face closed up and he spoke stiffly:

"I have always despised men who discuss the sexual peculiarities of their wives with other people. So let's drop it, shall we?" He glanced at his watch and picked up the phone. "Is there anything on my call? Nothing yet? All right."

He poured himself another drink. He watched the phone as though it were some stubborn, living creature which refused to follow orders. As the minutes passed, Carol became nervous and fidgety; his worry was so great that she thought of giving him the number of Joe's private cabin: 394 ring one. Yes, that might be a way of avoiding the informer's stigma. But she didn't want to risk it.

"Why are you worried?" she asked. "She was all right when I left her."

Dee regarded his visitor with interest. "What was she doing?"

"Uh ... getting ready for bed."

"Drinking?"

"Not seriously."

He lost some of his tautness, but returned his attention to the phone. She stood up. "I guess I'll get a room and go to bed. I'm too tired to start back now."

He spoke without looking at her. "I've got two beds. Take one. You won't bother me."

"I'm so happy to hear that," she said.

The sarcasm floated over his head. He was barricaded behind his worry, no better company than the silent telephone. She walked to the open space between the beds, took off the white cashmere sweater she wore over her halter, and untied the wrap-around skirt that covered her shorts. She was untying the halter when Dee finally noticed what she was doing.

"You could change in the bathroom," he said.

"I could, but there's no point in it. I always sleep raw anyway." She leaned over and let the halter fall into her hands. "Does it bother you?" she asked, looking at him.

She had his attention now, she saw that. No blazing passion in his eyes, though; just a look of mild interest. She knew her breasts were good, perhaps the best part of her; two rounded cones thrusting out from her chest and tipped with a virginal pinkness. Smiling at him, she dropped the shorts to the floor, then peeled down the panties.

"You hold up surprisingly well," he said.

She looked at him curiously. The strong, rugged face, the big hands loosely gripping his knees, made her feel soft and weak inside. "Under what?" she asked.

"Under a succession of men." He added quickly, "I meant no offense. But you haven't changed much in fifteen years. Not since ... that time we drove to the game at State, you and Marian and I. Remember? You got drunk and came into my room thinking it was your own, and stripped off your clothes?"

"I remember," she said, walking over to him. "And I wasn't as drunk as you thought I was."

He raised his brows, then smiled slowly. "I've often wondered what would have happened if Marian hadn't come looking—"

"I'd have crawled into bed with you." She moved forward until her knees touched his. "She won't come now."

"No." His hands closed on her knees, then began climbing her legs, kneading her thighs and sending tiny arrows of delight into the pit of her stomach. She leaned forward and kissed him, feeling his lips open under hers. She leaned back and squeezed his shoulders. "I was too drunk last night, darling. I can't remember enough of it."

"My call ..."

"You can hear the phone." She opened his pajamas and rubbed her palms over his naked chest and stomach. When he was ready she straddled his lap, paused for a brief, fumbling moment, then sank down with a low moan of pleasure. His arms around her, pressing her to him, flattening her breasts against his chest. He lay back on the bed, pulling her with him.

So much better sober, she thought. I can control it now, each little sensation, each little twinge of pleasure inside me. I am as much to him now as his wife could ever be, maybe more ...

She raised herself on her arms and looked down at him, still moving slowly. His eyes were open. For a long time she looked into his eyes, trying to read the thought behind them, to anticipate the direction of his pleasure. It was a strange and fascinating experience, looking down at this huge, rugged male who lay beneath her like a vanquished gladiator. Though she was serving him, she was at the same time ruling him, using his flesh for her own pleasure ... His chest began to heave. He squeezed his eyes shut and knotted his jaw muscles. He gave a low moan which might have been mistaken for a moan of pain. His fingers dug into her buttocks. She felt his thrusting strength, then a shiver crawled up her spine and left her weak and boneless. She collapsed upon his chest and sank her teeth into his neck, crying softly as convulsions of sweet agony racked her body...

Afterward she lay wrapped in a lethargy like a thick cotton blanket. As though from a great distance she heard him sit up and lift the phone, heard his voice: "Operator, is there anything on my call? Nothing? Thank you."

So much for that, she thought wryly. This is all I'll get from Dee, so I may as well be satisfied with it...

Lewis felt his skin crawl with impatience. For two hours he had been sitting in Marian's darkened house and waiting for her. He hadn't expected her to be gone so long; now he began to wonder if she would come back at all. Maybe she would stay all night with Joe, the man who sold boats ...

The vision brought a sour, bitter taste to his mouth. He gripped his right hand with his left and squeezed until the knuckles crackled. To think of Joe, the great lover of women, in bed with Marian, running his hands over the smooth flesh, the flesh of his woman—

Hell, I should kill them both. I should kill him right before her eyes. I could force her to watch it, and I'd do it very, very slowly ...

Unable to sit still, he got up and prowled the darkened room, probing the bookcases, rummaging in the liquor cabinet. He gave a start of surprise when his hand touched cold metal. "Well, I'll be—a gun!" He searched further, found the cartridges, and stuck both gun and ammunition in his pocket. He had no use for the gun, but he couldn't leave it with Marian. She might get hysterical and forget herself. She hated him; he had seen that tonight. Her hatred puzzled him, but it wasn't really important. Women had hated him before, then had come to love him. Or at least to stop fighting him, which came down to the same thing ...

With the gun weighting his pocket, Lewis felt more secure. He walked into Marian's bedroom and switched on her dressing table lamp. The heady smell of her perfume quickened his pulse. He went to the bed, turned back the rumpled coverlet, and pressed his nose to the sheet. He could smell the odor of her body still lingering where she had slept. He straightened and thought: if she were lying there now, open and waiting for him, the way it had been up on the ridge ...

But she was with Joe, the seller of boats. He felt the rage rise up and squeeze his throat. He looked around the room, clenching his fists, seeking an outlet for his wrath. There, on the dressing table Marian and that husband of hers shared a double frame of gold. Marian seemed to be looking straight at Lewis, taunting him with parted lips. For a second they seemed to quirk in a sarcastic smile—

"Bitch!" he shouted. "Dirty bitch!"

He swung his hand and knocked the picture from the dresser. Glass shattered. He tore her picture from the frame and ripped it in two, right down the middle of her taunting smile. Still his anger boiled. He swept his arm across the dressing table, sending lipstick, talcum, perfume, cologne, powder, all crashing to the floor. A cologne bottle shattered and filled the room with the reek of violets. A box of talcum powder split, sent up a choking aromatic cloud. Lewis jerked out her dresser drawers and flung her clothing around the room. He ran to her closet, pulled suits and dresses from the hangers, flung them to the floor. He picked up her laundry bag and carried it to the center of the room. By this time he was panting and perspiring. His shoes crunched on broken glass and made damp tracks in the cologne. He dumped the dirty clothes to the floor, reached inside, and felt one small, remaining garment ...

Marian's, he thought. He took out the wisp of nylon and bunched it in his fist, feeling the fabric spring back against his fingers. He thought of the garment containing the tender, trembling buttocks, clinging to her intimate flesh. Reverently, he touched it to his lips, folded it, then stuck it in his pocket.

His rage at Marian was gone now. He picked up the

pieces of her picture and put them carefully in his pocket. Later he would buy some Scotch tape and put her smile together again ...

He left the house and climbed the ridge, ducking and running through the low brush, moving as silently as an animal. During the last few days he had come to know the night as well as he knew the day. He found his boat, pushed off, and steered for the dam. When he was nearly there, he swerved and headed toward a long fishing dock. He cut his motor and read the words painted on the twelve-foot sign: *JOE FORREST—Marine sales and service.* Half a dozen new cabin cruisers rocked gently as the wake from Lewis' boat reached the dock. The house on the hill behind the dock was dark, the garage empty. Lewis didn't know where Joe was; only that Marian was with him...

Abruptly all his bitter anger flooded back. He set his oars in the oarlocks and rowed silently to the first of the cabin cruisers, tied his line to the ladder, and climbed aboard. The smell of new leather reached his nostrils as he entered the cabin. He took out the Mexican knife he had bought in San Antonio, pressed the release, and flicked open the curved, razor-edged blade. He drew it across the softly glowing leather of the seats, smiling as the padding puffed out through the incisions. Next he cut the steering cables and gouged long slashes in the rich paneling. When that was finished, he moved quietly to the next boat and did the same.

It took a half an hour to operate on all the boats. When he returned to his craft, Lewis felt an intense personal satisfaction. It would cost Joe Forrest several thousand dollars to get those boats ready to sell again. Marian would be the most expensive piece he'd ever enjoyed.

Lewis rowed a hundred yards off, started his motor, and set a course for a sign which flared red against the night sky:

MAC'S FLOATING PIZZA PALACE
BEER—WINE—COLD DRINKS
Race your motor for dockside service

Lewis pulled in fast, slammed his engine into reverse, and came to rest gently against the dock. A little blonde in tight shorts trotted toward him. Her small, immature breasts jiggled inside a jersey which carried the words: *MAC'S PIZZA*.

"Hi, Lewis. Want something?"

He regarded her thoughtfully. She was a high-school girl doing summer work; she seemed friendly enough, but he hadn't yet probed the depth of her friendship. And now, with pain squeezing his groin and fire gnawing at his vitals, he couldn't risk another frustration.

"Tell Marge to come out," he said.

She turned and walked away, tight-muscled little buttocks thrusting against her shorts. Lewis watched and squeezed the wheel until his knuckles turned white.

Then he saw Marge. She was a blonde too, but older than the normal run of summer help. She was a local girl, having come down from the wooded hills around the dam. During the winter she hopped tables in a honky-tonk in nearby Grady. She had large breasts, wide hips, and a face which was attractive in a heavy-featured way. Lewis had taken her out before. She was easy; there would be no delay with her ...

"Lewis. Haven't seen you for days."

Smile, Lewis. Certain preliminaries to be gotten out of the way.

Feeling the pressure grow inside, he asked: "You doing anything after work?"

Her face showed eagerness, quickly masked. "A guy is taking me to the Bar-C for a drink."

"I'll buy you beer and sandwiches."

"Just like that, you'll buy me beer and sandwiches. What about him?"

"Tell him you have a headache. Or a dose. Who cares?"

"Why should I?" She hunkered down beside the boat, elbows on knees, thighs swelling out below her shorts. "You don't come around for a week and then you expect me to go with you. You knock me out, Lewis, you really do."

He gazed down at the front of her blouse at the breasts hanging there like ripe, swollen fruit from a tree. His skin crawled with impatience, he wanted to seize her and yank her into his boat. Damn it, if she only knew how much he needed her now. She would come anyway; she only wanted to be coaxed. And, since the lights were bright and people were near, he saw no way of avoiding it...

"You look really sharp tonight, Marge. I'd forgotten how good you looked." Smiling, he put his hand into the blouse and pushed it down into the valley between her breasts.

"Lewis, not out here in public."

Even as she protested, she leaned forward to allow him greater freedom. He turned his hand over and let the heavy warmth of her breast lie in his palm. "Let's go somewhere private, then."

"After I get off ..."

"Now!" He moved his hand and felt the gentle thrust of the nipple. Her lips drooped at the comers and glistened wet in the light.

"Yes. All right. I'll tell Mac—"

She was back in five minutes, wearing a skirt and sweater against the night air. "Hurry," she said. "I don't want to be seen leaving." Lewis roared off so fast his prow pointed toward the rising half-moon. When he leveled off and began to plane, he pointed the nose toward the low, forested mass which marked the uninhabited south shore of the lake.

"Hey! Where are you going?"

"To get some privacy."

"But you said a sandwich and a beer—"

"They'll taste better later."

"I'm hungry now."

"You'll be hungrier later."

"Lewis, I don't mind being nice to you. You know that. But if you think you can just pick me up and five minutes later, wham-bam, you've got the wrong girl."

He glanced over at her, saw the face white in the moonlight, the wind blowing her hair off her forehead and moulding the sweater against her breasts. Her mouth was a tight line, and Lewis thought: maybe she means it, maybe she'll fight ...

He aimed toward the black shadow which marked an isolated cove.

"Lewis, I mean it. I won't!"

"Won't what?"

"I won't let you."

He laughed, feeling the hot pulse of excitement in his loins. He opened the throttle and grinned into the wind.

A minute later his keel grated on the rocky beach. Lewis jumped out with the rope and pulled, using the tardy swell of his own wake to get his boat safely beached. He tied it to a low branch and looked at Marge sitting in the boat, her arms clasped around her waist

"Are you getting out?"

"No. I told you."

Lewis sat down on a rock and lit a cigarette,

watching her and trying to decide what he'd do to her. He could do whatever he wanted here on this lonely and desolate shore.

"Lewis, take me home."

A few minutes later she said, her voice faintly whining: "Are you just going to sit here?"

"That's up to you."

Another minute passed, then she asked in a subdued voice, "Have you got a match?"

"Come and get it."

"Oh, damn you, Lewis ..." The boat rocked as she stood up.

"Bring a couple of those life preserver cushions, too."

Sighing, she picked up the cushions and stepped ashore. She tossed a cushion down beside him and sat on it. She leaned toward him with a cigarette between her lips, holding the pose until he lit it for her.

"Well," she said after a long drag, "here I am. Now what?"

Lewis was displeased with her. She was giving in too easily; maybe the high-school girl would have been better. True, Marge's voice was heavy with sarcasm, but beneath it she was as willing as he was; she only wanted to have her ego fed. Lewis knew exactly how to get her eager cooperation, but cooperation wasn't what he needed tonight.

"Take off your clothes," he said.

"Oh, now wait a minute, Lewis—"

"Strip. Or I'll leave you here."

At that moment an owl chose to give a sepulchral hoot somewhere in the forested hills behind them. It seemed to symbolize the loneliness of the place. Marge stood up, peeled off her sweater, unzipped the shorts, then stopped. Her voice sounded almost tearful:

"Lewis, why do you act like this? You know I don't

mind if I'm treated right. I'm just as ready as the next—"

"Go on!" he said hoarsely. "Get done with it."

Quickly she dropped the shorts then unbuttoned the blouse and took it off. She bent to put it on the ground, her breasts swinging inside the hammock of her brassiere. The moon-shadowed cleft looked like a smear of ink. She straightened and reached back for the clasp, saying:

"You always helped me before. I don't know what's got into you—"

"Don't talk. Just do as you're told."

"Oh, hell!" She jerked off the brassiere and her breasts swelled free in the moonlight; white globes tipped with darkness, like an over-exposed photo. Then her panties joined the rest of her discarded clothing and she kneeled beside him. He felt her arm slide around his shoulder, breasts pressing against him. "Kiss me, honey. Warm me up. It will be so much easier, so much better..."

He swung his arm and knocked her sprawling on the rocky bank. She lay like a capsized turtle, all four limbs in the air. He stood up and looked down at her. "Did I tell you to do that?"

"No, but I thought—" Her throat caught in a sob. "Lewis, you're acting crazy! Tell me what to do. I'll do it, then you can take me home."

He pulled Marian's panties from his pocket and tossed them onto her stomach. "Put them on."

She shoved her feet inside them, braced her heels and raised her hips off the ground while she drew them up to her waist. Then she lowered herself to the ground and looked up at him, silently waiting for orders. This, thought Lewis, would make up for the frustration of the evening. She wasn't Marian, but she would serve ...

He bent over and hooked his fingers beneath the elastic band. He jerked upward, heard a stretching rip mingled with Marge's thin little cry of fear and surprise. He straightened and saw that the top part had torn away while the rest of it still clung to her body. He bent and tore away the remnant of nylon while Marge lay like a dead body. When it was gone, he knew he was ready; so ready he couldn't wait another second. He bent down. He heard Marge gasp, then: "Look—"

"Shut up!" Lewis smelled the stale-beer, barmaid odor of her body. If not for that, he could have pretended she was Marian.

"Lewis, you're not! Stop a minute, *please!* No, no don't—"

Her fists beat against his shoulders; her legs pinched together; her hips writhed and twisted as she tried to evade him. He stretched his arm behind him, closed his hand on a heavy rock, lifted it, and brought it down hard on her forehead. She stiffened, suddenly, and every muscle in her body went hard and rigid as steel. Then she gave a shuddering gasp and her body went slack ...

Lewis arose, his passion gone, and looked at the girl. He felt a chill of fright. God, blood running out of her head like black soot. Eyes open. Shouldn't be open; Jesus, I got excited and hit her too damn hard ...

He ran down the bank, and dipped up a double handful of water, ran back and threw it on her face. She did not move. He ran again, then again. How many trips? How many times had he run down and back, fighting the knowledge, patting those cheeks which shivered under his hands like a cut of meat, getting colder and colder all the time ...

She was dead.

For a long time he sat looking at her. An icy calmness

came over him. He gathered her clothes, carried them up the bank, and buried them in a hole which he gouged out with a stick. He covered the hole with rocks, then carried the limp body to the boat. He found a large rock and threw that in too. He rowed out into the lake, cut off a piece of his tow-line, and knotted it around her waist until it sank deeply into her flaccid belly. He tied the other end around the rock, rolled her over the side, and threw the rock in behind her.

Alibi, he thought as he roared across the silvery surface of the lake. Maybe somebody saw me at Mac's; got to find out ...

The high-school girl came out, looking tired. "We're just closing up. I thought—where's Marge?"

"I was supposed to pick her up here after work."

"She's not here. I haven't seen her since right after she talked to you."

"When did she leave?"

"Wait a minute." She went inside and returned a minute later. "Mac said she took off early, with a headache."

Lewis felt a flood of relief. He was in the clear. Then he remembered and tried to look unhappy. "Damn. First time I've been stood up for ... a long time." He looked at the girl, noticing the virginal breasts nudging the fabric of her shirt. "Get in. I can give you a lift home."

"I'm meeting a guy ... tonight."

He understood the pause. "Tomorrow night?"

"Maybe. See me before ten. 'Bye now." She walked away, the piston-throb of her little buttocks straining against the shorts. Tomorrow, he thought, easing out into the lake. Maybe I'll get Marian and maybe I won't. If I don't, this little girl will be next ...

At home he slept peacefully for the first time in a week.

6

Joe Forrest opened his eyes, then squeezed them shut against the pain of the morning light. He moved his hand, felt the warm naked body beside him, and drew it away sharply.

Ah, morning. He hated the morning, particularly when he had to deal with a new woman. They were always the most difficult in the mornings. Some were imperiously demanding, expecting him to crawl at their feet because they had climbed into his bed the night before. Others tried to pry loose his protective shell and probe the secret of the inner man, as though their brief intimacy had given them a permanent place in his private life. Some became teary and guilt-stricken, anxious to get back to their husbands and start making amends, cursing Joe as a homewrecker because they had answered the call of their own rampant estrogens. And the worst ones pulled out pictures of the kiddies and dared him to contradict when they said they weren't fit mothers.

To tell the truth, Joe Forrest hated women. And in the morning, when they were at their most hateworthy, his only defense was a deeply ingrained ritual which got them out of bed, fed, and back to their homes with a minimum of anger and recrimination.

He stretched out his hand and flicked the switch which would start the coffee pot in the kitchen. He reached for a cigarette, lit it, and drew the smoke into his lungs. Only then did he turn to look at his sleeping companion. For a second he could not remember who she was; only that he had done well for himself. Her nude back was golden and smoothly rounded, and her bright gold hair was delightfully tousled on the pillow.

Yes. Marian, wife of the lawyer, the woman he had watched every summer for the last four years. He had been afraid he would never get her, because she and her husband had seemed happy together. But this summer he had seen the shifting glance in her eyes which marked the beginning of discontent. Two weeks ago she had given him a searching, piercing look which seemed to strip him bare and expose his manhood for her inspection; a look as significant of readiness as the red rose in a Mexican girl's hair, or four knots in the turban of a West Indian woman. And so, here was Marian.

Gently he raised the sheet and exposed the rest of her back. Soft, padded valley of spine shallowing slightly as it descended into the stark whiteness which began at her waist, white bulge of buttocks rounded off into nothing because her legs were drawn under her. He felt a sharp urge to awaken her with a tender pinch where the skin drew tightest, but that would be a violation of routine. First came the coffee, then the morning session, then breakfast and a light, friendly goodbye. No use tampering with a good, workable system.

A toneless *ping* from the kitchen told him the coffee was ready. He got up, slipped on a bathrobe, padded into the kitchen. He fixed the tray without even thinking about it; the accessories were already in the refrigerator, placed there the previous afternoon by his cleaning woman: sugar, cream, two halved grapefruits heaped with sugar. He poured the coffee from the electric percolator into the silver server, put it on the tray, then arranged cups and accessories beside it. Finished, he regarded the tray with a faint dissatisfaction. The routine treatment did not seem quite right; the fruit of four years' ripening deserved something extra. Yes, she had been drinking last night, probably had a fuzzy hangover ...

He broke two eggs, poured the whites into the blender, added a dash of tabasco sauce, three squirts of seltzer, a shot of vodka, tossed in a half cup of tomato juice, and turned on the motor. A minute later he poured the frothy pink liquid into a tall glass, put it on the tray, and carried it into the bedroom.

The bed was empty.

"Marian?" he called. No answer.

He set the tray on the nightstand and peered into the bathroom. Not there. What the hell—?

He ran to the window and looked out. She was a hundred yards away, walking down the graveled lane in the first slanting rays of the sun. She looked like a funny, shapely tramp in her blue jeans and flannel shirt. Joe ran to the door and opened it.

"Hey! Come back here."

She hesitated, walked on a few more steps, then stopped and turned. "I've got to get home."

"I'll take you, for God's sake! You don't have to walk."

She came toward him like a shy animal approaching a waterhole. Then she stopped again. "Right away. My husband might have come back unexpectedly."

She looked pale and wan without makeup, almost frightened. Joe felt sorry for her. "Look, call your house. If he answers, hang up. Then you can start making up a story. If he doesn't answer, well, you've got nothing to worry about."

She started walking back to the house. Joe turned and stepped inside the house. He was upset, not only by the violation of routine, but because it looked as though he would lose out on the morning session. He fidgeted in the bedroom and heard her finger the telephone dial, waited for the sound of her voice, then heard the click as she replaced the receiver. She came into the room looking relieved. "Nobody home. What's this?" She nodded at the frothy pink glass.

"For you. If you've got a hangover."

"A slight tingle, yes." She lifted the glass, drained it, and said, "Good."

There was a faint pink dew on her upper lip. He drew out his handkerchief and dabbed at it, then circled her in his arms and kissed her. She accepted him passively for a second, then pushed him away, gently but firmly, and picked up the coffee tray. "Let's have it in the kitchen, shall we?"

Joe followed, feeling more upset than ever. First she had tried to run away, then she had given him the cold shoulder; now she was leading him around in his own house. His hope for a morning session dwindled to a pinpoint.

Over coffee he studied her across the table. The hangover remedy had brought a touch of color to her cheeks, and something else had smoothed out the tense lines around her mouth. She had not fastened the top two buttons of her flannel shirt, and he could see the deepening shadow between her breasts. He felt desire strike like a sudden knife-thrust into his loins. He pushed away his coffee, got up and walked around the table, and rested his hands on her shoulders.

"Let's go back to bed."

"You promised to take me home."

"I will, later," he said.

"Now."

"Kiss me first."

She turned up her face and he bent to touch her soft, cool lips. He slid his hand inside the shirt and palmed a breast cupped by the brassiere.

"Joe, that isn't necessary."

"Necessary?" He moved his hand, forcing it inside the brassiere, touching the warm, trembling flesh. "I don't know what you mean."

"I'm aware of your reputation for virility. It isn't necessary to prove it by exploits this morning." She seized his wrist and pulled at his hand with a strength which told him her protest was genuine. Disappointed, he left her and returned to his chair. He never pushed himself beyond the first protest although his restraint was more practical than gallant. Force always increased resistance, while a show of indifference often became a challenge to a woman.

He poured her a second cup of coffee. "I'm sorry you didn't get much from it last night."

Her tone was gently scolding. "I didn't say that, Joe."

"Well—you don't want a repeat."

"No."

"There you are. Why should you object, after last night, unless you didn't enjoy it."

"No, now listen." She fingered the rim of her cup. "I am grateful for what you did last night. I had been curious for a long time. I wanted to know ... how it would be to hold another man and let him make love to me. Now I know. So why repeat?"

He felt prickly and uncomfortable; he wasn't sure he liked what this woman was telling him, but he admired her sharp, frank attitude behind it. So many of those pretty ones had minds like bread dough, minds that gave under the pressure of new ideas, then oozed slowly back into their original shape. Joe wondered why he had never noticed Marian's intelligence before. Perhaps because she had been too near her husband; so many women blanked out their brains when they were around their husbands ...

"You're staring, Joe. What do you see?"

He wrinkled his brow. "An enigma. If you liked it last night, why do you object to doing it again?"

"What happened last night doesn't justify throwing

myself away this morning."

"Then you didn't like it?"

"You're deliberately misunderstanding, Joe. Even if it had been the most beautiful experience in the world, I wouldn't want more of it now. It's a joy for five minutes, maybe ten, then it's over. And life has to go on."

"What kind of life?" As she raised her brows, puzzled, he added, "Look, I never break up a happy marriage. It's a rule of mine. That's why I never bothered you before. But this summer—"

"I know. However, it was my fault. And I can put a stop to it."

"Go back to the husband, shine his shoes, iron his clothes, kiss him—"

"Don't be sarcastic, Joe. It isn't like you."

He felt a crawling frustration. He knew how to deal with tears, accusations, pictures of the kiddies—but this cool, thoughtful determination threw him. He stood up. "Listen, what the hell do you think I am? Some repairman? A plumber you call in to fix a leaky faucet, then when everything's running good, it's thank you very much, and send me a bill. Don't you think you owe me something?"

She was silent a moment. "Yes, I suppose I do. What would you suggest?"

The question caught him by surprise. He looked into the green eyes and saw that she was serious. He took a deep breath, brushed back his hair, and tried to speak in a calm, unemotional voice. But his words came out in a hoarse whisper. "You know what I want."

"All right." She rose from her chair, her fingers working at the buttons on her shirt. She walked toward the bedroom, letting the shirt drop from her shoulders. In the door she turned, the brassiere snow-white against her golden skin and taut with the thrust of her breasts. "But this is it, you understand? After this there's nothing between us."

"I understand," he whispered. And he followed her into the bedroom, feeling a strange weakness in his knees. He stood in the door and watched her finish undressing. When the last wisp of clothing was gone, she sat down on the edge of the bed, swung her legs up, and stretched out on her back. She looked up at him and smiled.

"It's all right, Joe. I don't mind doing it."

His hands fumbled at his bathrobe, his blood hammered against his temples. He lay down, trembling as he felt her warm flesh pressing against him. He kissed her, felt the soft parting of her lips. She moved her legs to accommodate him. His self-control was slipping away; he was like a teenager with his first woman. It was going to end too soon, too soon ... too soon ...

It wasn't yet eight o'clock when he turned up the gravel driveway to her cabin.

"Let me out here, Joe. I'll walk."

He stopped. "Look, Marian, I know we made a sort of a deal ..."

"Yes. The deal stands."

"But I don't want it that way. I want to see you again."

"I'm sorry, Joe." She held out her hand. "I've got to hold you to your promise. Goodbye."

Then she was gone, leaving him with a cool tingling in his palm where her hand had touched him. He watched her walk up the gravel road, her shapely buttocks playing beneath the blue jeans. Memory of their trembling under his palms brought a rush of blood to his temples. He turned his car around, spurting gravel. Maybe she was right in ending it. He had found himself growing interested in her mind, and that, for a freedom-loving bachelor, was a perilous interest indeed.

Joe was not the first to arrive at his dock. Kenneth, the high-school boy who pumped gas for him during the summer, met him at the gangplank. His adolescent face was grim and serious.

"Joe, you better brace yourself. Somebody tore hell out of those new cabin jobs."

Joe ran across the dock and mounted the ladder of a new 30-foot Chris-Craft. He gasped at the sight of the slashed upholstery, scarred woodwork, and the scattered viscera of the wiring. It was as though his own flesh had been scarred and torn, for Joe not only sold boats, he loved boats. Whoever had destroyed these beautiful things had to be insane with hatred. And Joe could not imagine who could hate him so passionately...

Joe said to Kenneth, "They all like this?"

"More or less. You want me to call the sheriff?"

Joe shook his head without even considering it. This was an act motivated by passion, not profit. That pointed to some insanely jealous husband, and he would have to deal with the man personally, not through the law.

"I'll get the insurance man over for an estimate," he told Kenneth. "You get back to the pumps. I'll be pretty busy today."

He walked off.

First, he thought as he inserted the key in his house door, I'll have to find out whose husband is most likely to have found out. Beginning with Marian.

He lifted the telephone.

She came on the line quavery and breathless. "Yes?" "Marian, can you talk?"

"Yes, Joe. Lord, it's terrible!"

"It is. Do you have any idea—?" Suddenly he realized

that she could know nothing about his boats. "What's terrible?"

"I came in and found the house in a mess. Bedroom torn apart, bottles broken, clothes strung all over the floor ... God, he must have come in after I left."

Joe gripped the phone tightly. "Who? You know who did it?"

"Yes. Or at least I'm pretty sure I do. It's the boy who drives a ski-boat for the resort. Lewis. He's been watching the house for the last few days, and I'm sure—"

"Wait. Wait!" Joe felt as though he were sinking into quicksand. "Marian, I want to get it straight. Start at the beginning. How'd you get tied up with this kook?"

"You remember I told you I'd been looking ... around?"

"Oh, Christ. Go on."

"I didn't know he was crazy at the time, and I thought, well ..."

As Joe listened to her story, he felt a shifting tide of emotions sweep over him. He felt a bittersweet regret that she had not come to him when the urge for adultery first had seized her. He felt anger and bitter self-contempt because she had come to him last night out of fear, not attraction. Last night seemed unsportsmanlike, a violation of his own code of ethics, like picking on a cripple. He felt the ground crumbling beneath his self-confidence. He had been so smug and self-satisfied—

When she finished, he said: "Listen, I'm going out to call on this kid. You go over to Carol's—

"She isn't home, Joe. She had a date last night ..."

"Oh. Well, lock yourself in the house. I'll be out as soon as I—"

"Joe, something else. Lewis has a gun."

Joe caught his breath in surprise. "Are you sure?"

"Yes. Dee left his automatic with me. It's gone now."

Joe felt a chill climb his spine. A madman with a gun; that was more than he had bargained for when he had picked Marian out of that crowd at the party. "Okay. Be careful about opening your door to anyone. Play it cool."

"You too, Joe. Be careful ... please!"

There was, he thought as he hung up the phone, a thrill in hearing a lovely woman say those words with just the right amount of fear and affection. It afforded a man some consolation...

Charley Barr, the man who ran the Pla-Mo Resort, shook his head when Joe asked about Lewis.

"You're three hours late. He got me out of bed at sun-up and said he was quitting. Wanted his pay."

Joe frowned. "Did he say what he planned to do?"

"Just that he'd decided to move on. I wasn't surprised. The kid drifted in out of nowhere a year ago. Now he's drifted out again. He wasn't worth a damn to me anyway, these last few days."

Joe left the resort, armed with the address of Lewis' boarding house. The landlady told him that the boy had moved out early that morning, bag and baggage, saying he had a job on an Arizona dude ranch. She was a squat, ugly woman whose frustrated maternal instinct had somehow become fixed on Lewis. She sighed heavily.

"I'll miss him," she said. "He was a nice, quiet boy, never threw parties in his room or tried to sneak in girls. Always paid on time—"

Joe interrupted her eulogy. "Any friends he might be staying with?"

"He didn't have any friends. Never got any mail. Had a girl who serves beer at Mac's. A white-trash girl from the hills named Marge. Lewis could have done better than that, a nice-looking, decent boy like him ..."

Joe left before he succumbed to the temptation to destroy her illusions about nice-looking boys. He used one of his own boats to reach the pizza palace, and there Lewis' trail dwindled to nothing. Mac was in his kitchen, shirt off, drinking a cup of coffee. He gave a disgusted snort when Joe asked about Marge.

"That dumb broad better not show her face around here again. She left me during the rush hour last night, and she isn't home yet."

"Would she have gone with Lewis?"

"Hell, yes, she'd have taken off with anyone, but especially Lewis. She has hot pants for that kid."

Back in his office, Joe called Marian and told her what he had learned, then cautioned: "You'd still better be damn careful. This boy's a weirdo, and they sometimes get smart ideas."

"Ideas?"

"Like pretending to leave, so you'll let your guard down. Don't do it."

"All right. I won't."

"And you'd better report that stolen gun, just in case he kills somebody with it." He paused, then: "You hear?"

"Yes, Betty. I certainly will do that. And we'll see you at the party."

Joe was urbane enough to understand why she had switched to calling him Betty. Her husband had come in. Joe hung up the phone and walked out on the dock. He thought of Dee alone with Marian, exercising those rights a husband has. He envied Dee. And that worried him, because he had never envied a married man before ...

He saw the insurance adjustor coming toward him with a pad and pen. Now, thought Joe, I'll find out what that night with her has cost me.

7

Dee watched his wife cradle the receiver and turn slowly to face him. He wanted to run forward and take her in his arms, stroke her hair and touch her body to verify the fact that she was safe and well. He felt a delicious relief from the fear which had tormented him ever since he had gotten his call through at five a.m. and had heard the phone ring endlessly in the empty house.

"Are you all right?" he asked.

"Of course, Dee," she said, smiling hesitantly. "What brings you back so early?"

He only looked at her, his nerves still taut from the ninety-mile-per-hour drive, his big hands still curved in the shape of his steering wheel. Replacing his fear, suspicion suddenly grew inside him.

"What have you been doing?"

"Nothing important. Waiting." She stood up and walked toward him, and he saw that she was still dressed for bed. Her quilted house-coat, belted loosely around the waist, fell back from the short frilly nightgown which reached only to the beginning of her long, brown thighs. She came up to him and put her hands on his shoulders: "Aren't you going to kiss me?"

He smelled the light bouquet of her perfume and the soft scent of woman-flesh still warm from the bed. It was all he could do to keep from seizing her and pulling her to him. "Were you home all night?"

"Of course, darling." She slid her arms around his neck and rocked against him. The thrust of her pelvis punctuated her next words: "And I missed you."

Still he stood with his arms at his sides. He now had two mysteries to solve: her failure to answer the phone, and her oddly affectionate welcome after the bitterness of their parting. He wished his mind were free of suspicion, so that he could give her the passion she seemed to want: but the questions would not be dislodged. Almost with regret, he asked: "Were you here at five this morning?"

She looked up at him with her green eyes wide. "Why, yes. Where else?"

"I called. You didn't answer."

She looked at him with a curiously blank expression. Then she turned away and walked to the kitchen table. "Dee, you're all tensed up. I'll make some coffee so you can relax."

"You haven't explained why you didn't answer the phone."

She moved slowly, opening the electric percolator and measuring out the coffee. "Darling, at five I was deeply sunk in sleep, I guess. I didn't hear a thing."

Her movements were calm and unhurried as she filled the pot with water, placed the coffee basket inside, and plugged the cord into the wall socket.

"It rang eighteen times," said Dee. "You always wake up before the third ring."

She laughed, and Dee thought he detected a high, false note, but he couldn't see her face to make sure.

"I'm afraid this was one of those times, darling, that I didn't wake up at all." She turned suddenly to face him, her hands braced against the cabinet behind her. "You imagine I was out with a man at that hour?"

Her question failed to register in Dee's mind, so wanton and seductive was her posture. The backward thrust of her shoulders drew the housecoat off her bosom, and he could see the pale rose nipples trembling against the thin gown, capping the white globes of her breasts. Her feet were planted widely apart, forcing up the hem of her nightgown and affording him a glimpse of a dark-gold color that was neither flesh nor fabric. He knew she was exposing herself deliberately, and that made it all the more exciting.

His throat was tight when he spoke: "I don't ignore the possibility."

"Dee, darling, don't be silly." She moved her hips against the cabinet as she spoke, drawing his attention to the tender juncture of leg and torso. "I was lonely and I took too many drinks. I got morbid and restless, so I took a seconal to help me sleep. Apparently I slept too well. I'm sorry if you got all upset." She pushed herself away and came toward him with an unMarian-like sway to her hips. She began loosening his tie. "Why don't you make yourself comfortable and get in bed? I'll bring you coffee and we'll talk."

Dee stood still as she took off his tie, then his jacket, and started on the buttons of his shirt. Her explanation about the seconal seemed reasonable, yet he couldn't help wishing she had mentioned it first, without hesitation. It had seemed too much like an afterthought, a tardy dissimulation.

Still, with her hair tickling his nose, and her soft hands moving inside the shirt and caressing his bare chest, he found it hard to concentrate on the inconsistencies of her story. Here was a wife who had been turning cold for months; suddenly she was acting like a sex-hungry teenager. Dee was not a man to let the unexpectedness of a gift spoil his appreciation of it. He looked down and saw her moist lips parted slightly; he kissed her and felt her hips tilt upward in a sudden, delicious invitation. He pulled loose the belt of her housecoat and threw it open, then the warmth of her body returned to his, softer and more intimate than before. He sent his hands around her waist and felt the nightgown slide beneath his palms, as though it were a film of oil coating her skin. He enclosed a globe of her buttocks with each hand and felt her muscles jump to a quivering rigidity against his palms. She began moving slowly, clinging to him from breast to knee.

The banked fire of his passion rose high and throbbed against his temples. In a remote part of his mind, he felt a pleased surprise at the resurgence of his manhood. He would not have thought it possible after being with Carol—she had resembled a starving animal, hungry for him, demanding that he fill the aching emptiness of her lean, lithe body. Now, he discovered that satiety for one woman does not always carry over to another. The affair with Carol, for all its fire, had been an awkward fumbling with an unfamiliar body. Now his manhood, having visited a strange port, ached to return to the familiar hollows of Marian's flesh; hands thirsted to enclose the breasts whose shape he knew so well...

"Let's go," he said.

She drew away from him, her cheeks bright and her voice quick and breathless. "Yes. Get undressed and into bed. Relax ... then it'll be better. I'll bring coffee."

In the bedroom, Dee found that his hands trembled as he disrobed. For a moment he considered the explanation she had given him; there was a hole in it somewhere, but his brains were too jumbled to find it now. The hell with it. That could wait. She was coming to him in a few seconds ...

He lay on the bed and called, "Marian!"

He heard her footsteps, then she came through the door. "What?"

"Forget the coffee. I'll relax later."

Without hesitation, as though she had been expecting his request, she shrugged the robe from her shoulders and let it drop to the floor. She looked at him questioningly, a tiny glint of moisture on her lower lip. "Shall I pull the curtain?"

He felt his pulse leap with excitement. Always before, on the rare occasions when they made love during the day, she had insisted on pulling the curtain. At night she turned out the light. Now, as she stood waiting for his answer, he saw that she was standing in a patch of sunlight that came through the window. The sun pierced the nightgown as though it were film, and he thought: God, is this wanton woman my wife? Her face was full and bright with color, the lines of tension gone. Where had those lines gone—and why? Another puzzle for later consideration...

"Don't pull the curtain," he said through dry lips. "Unless you want to."

She smiled mischievously, wetting her lips with a pink tongue. "You want to watch?"

"Yes."

With a smooth, confident movement, she pulled loose the drawstring which held the gown at her throat. She caught the hem and raised it slowly to reveal the sudden whiteness of her hips and the flat stomach broken by the tender cup of her navel. Her breasts came up with the nightgown, then fell back into place as she freed them from the gown. Then it was off over her head, leaving her hair tousled and hoydenish. As she tossed the garment carelessly behind her, Dee made another discovery. From where he lay, he could see a second Marian in the mirror on the dressing table—the fine straight line of her back, the snowy bulge of her buttocks. And he saw himself lying on the bed, his arms behind his head and his feet stretched out before him. He thought: now I see why some people put mirrors in their bedrooms; it would be exciting as hell just to lie here and have her come to him...

"Come here," he said.

"In a minute, darling." She smiled at him. "It will be better in a minute."

She placed her palms flat against her hips and pushed them slowly down to her knees as though divesting herself of some invisible garment. She drew her fingers up the inner softness of her thighs, then touched herself in a way that made him gasp with surprise. This could not be his wife; she was a creature possessed by Aphrodite, dedicated to the worship of love. She was looking at him through eyes bright and unseeing; she caressed herself as though she lay alone in some deep forest glen...

"Come here," he said again.

She didn't answer. He saw the gleam of sweat on her forehead, and the bright flare of color on her cheeks. Her thighs trembled as she moved. Dee knew there was only one thing to do: seize the trembling flesh and direct this wanton, wasted passion toward himself. He had to fill the warm chalice of her sex before she quenched the fire herself.

He rolled off the bed and walked to her, his knees stiff, carpet tickling his bare feet. She gave a soft sigh when he reached her, then she slid her arms around his neck and fell backward to the carpet, pulling him with her. Dee thought of moving to the bed, but Marian seemed unaware that she had fallen: the engine of her sex had never stopped working. Now it speeded up, and her breath came in quick little gasps. Briefly she seemed to become aware of Dee; she paused just for a second, lifted herself from the floor to give him easier access, then resumed her movement. But now it was different; now he was a part of the machine, meshing and blending with her, the rod and the socket, the shaft and the gear, twisting and turning in a union which was less like love than like the silent, desperate combat of two fierce animals bent on destroying each other. Then abruptly they achieved a unity, a harmony too perfect to be machinelike. Now they were parts of a single living organism. All the long years their bodies had known each other had been only a tentative groping toward this moment, a rehearsal for this, the real performance. And then the play reached its peak. Dee felt the clawing of her hands, the tension of her joints as though she were being stretched on a rack. He glimpsed her face and saw her twisted, shapeless mouth and her neck cords taut like wire and her lips curling back from her teeth and he thought: this isn't counterfeit, this is real.

Objectivity ended there. Tender perfumed jaws seized him and twisted, and his brain held only one thought, to drive, to lose himself inside this woman, to surround himself totally with soft, throbbing flesh...

Afterward he sat back on his haunches and listened to the bubbling hiss of her breath between her teeth.

"Ah, husband, husband..." She said. She lay exactly as he had left her, her body seeming to flow out and spread over the carpet. "I feel as if... as if somebody has taken all the bones out of my body and left just the flesh and the skin."

He kissed her soft, wet mouth, then rose and went to the bed. All the tension had left him; he lay half-conscious and listened to her rise and go to the bathroom. Minutes later he felt the bed sag as she sat down beside him. He forced one eye open and saw that she was holding out a steaming cup of black coffee. She was still nude; her nipples were sunken slightly into the rose-tan aureoles; her breasts no longer thrust upward, but seemed to relax and fill the convex cups of their lower sides. Looking at her, he felt like a mountain climber gazing back at the peak from which he had just descended and saying to himself: *I climbed to that airy place. I planted my staff there.*

He pushed himself up and took the coffee. It was several minutes before he spoke, then: "That's never happened before. Maybe I should leave for the night more often."

She lit a cigarette and gave it to him before answering. "You don't have to leave. It will happen again."

"You have decided that?"

"Let's say I've learned something."

"How?"

"Don't question it, husband. Accept it." She got up and drew the curtains, throwing the room into twilight. She came back to the bed and took his empty cup, and her body was a pale shape against the deeper shadows. "That is, unless you have some criticism."

"No criticism," he said.

And yet, after she left him, the questions bubbled up in his mind. Why her sudden change? Had this morning's wanton display been a deliberate pose to put off his suspicion that she'd been with a man the night before? If so, she was one hell of a performer; he had never known anyone to successfully counterfeit that final, sobbing convulsion. Well, then, what had changed her? It could still have been another man who had awakened her to the potential pleasure in her body. This thought tore Dee's mind in two. One part said, accept—accept this new woman. The other part was filled with a sour, bitter jealousy; it shattered his ego to think that another man could succeed where he had failed. As he dropped off to sleep, his head swirled with a vision of Marian lying nude in someone else's arms, breasts sweating, teeth nibbling the stranger's shoulder...

When Dee got up he found more food for suspicion.

Her bedroom had a clean, scrubbed smell, but it failed to mask an unaccustomed reek of perfume and cologne. The glass was missing from the frame of their wedding picture, and her figure was gone. She explained that the storm had blown open a window, knocking the picture and a bottle of cologne to the floor. He might have accepted that if he had not known that the storm had come up from the southwest, and her bedroom was on the northeast corner. He checked further, his mind now unclouded by passion or fatigue. He felt as though he were once again a prosecuting attorney collecting evidence, arranging and sorting the pieces of the puzzle. He would make no accusation until he could confront her with a case so detailed and airtight that she could deny nothing. But the absence of the gun, and her explanation that she had thrown it into the lake because it frightened her, jarred him so greatly that he could no longer contain his questions:

"Look, Marian, if you were afraid of the gun, why didn't you just throw away the cartridges?"

"I didn't think of that," she said, her face peaceful. She was sewing on a dress for Sharon, and the scene was as domestic as potatoes and gravy.

"Oh, come on, Marian." He paced the room, cracking his knuckles. "Tell me what really happened. You stepped out of the house for a little while and someone broke in and stole it. Right?"

"I wasn't out of the house, Dee."

"Marian, if the gun was stolen I have to report it. It's registered in my name."

"Then report it stolen if you want to."

"But *was* it stolen? That's what I want to know."

"Dee, I told you—!"

"Then where did you throw it? I'll put on my mask and dive for it."

"I don't remember, Dee. I don't remember!" Her nose reddened and moisture glinted on her lashes. Suddenly she threw down her sewing and jumped up. "You're spoiling everything with your silly suspicions. And it started to be ... wonderful..."

She went into her bedroom and slammed the door. Dee looked out across the quiet water and had the strange wish that Marian could have been clever enough to carry it off without arousing his suspicion. He thought: We don't hate our mates for cheating. We hate them for being careless enough for us to catch them. I know the gun is not in the lake. I know the wind did not destroy the picture, and I know that she was not in the house at five this morning ...

He called his assistant and learned that Barry had presented Dee's brief on the Tasty-Dip case, and the court had recessed for two days. There was nothing to take him back to the city, so Dee decided to stay and go to Carol's party that night. He did not care for parties. He was not sure whether Carol was celebrating the anniversary of one of her divorces, or of one of her marriages. Marian had accepted the invitation more than two weeks before, and in any case, the noise next door would make it impossible to relax at home. Besides, the party might supply a clue to Marian's mysterious behavior.

They arrived at eight. Dee made a polite round of greeting, then sat in a corner sipping vodka martinis and watching Marian. She was like a woman with a high fever. Her eyes were bright, her cheeks flushed. She talked gaily and laughed often. She was wearing a black cocktail dress of some elastic material that clung to her flat stomach and hugged the opposing roundnesses of breast and buttock. Dee noticed how the men clustered around her; he was torn between pride that she was his woman and the nagging suspicion that she was also someone else's.

Carol hovered over him possessively. She kept his glass filled, and with each refill would press her leg against his or let her breast brush his shoulder. Dee thought it must be obvious that they had slept together; she might as well have worn a sign on her back saying: *DEE IS MY LOVER*. Then he thought: if Carol shows her feelings about me, why wouldn't Marian show them about her own lover? He began looking for signs passing between Marian and the men on hand, a search which became an obsession as the vodka martinis, pressed upon him by Carol, bounced into his stomach and sent their swirling fumes into his brain. The green mold of suspicion thickened and spread as he catalogued the males around her.

Carl Sanborn, real estate dealer. He told dirty jokes and whispered the four-letter words so that Marian had to lean forward to hear, and sometimes to ask for a repeat. Carl was short, obese. At some point in every party he would throw up in the bathroom and then pass out on the terrace. Marian couldn't have been that desperate. Dee wouldn't insult her by suspecting Carl...

Gary Bailey, insurance man, let his hand rest too long on Marian's shoulder and talked too intimately into her ear. She laughed and shook her head without looking at him. Bailey was a flirt who propositioned every woman he met after his third drink. After five drinks he even propositioned his wife. None of the women took Bailey seriously; he found his extra-curriculum sex in the blaring honky-tonks down at the dam, and he usually paid cash for the privilege. Mark him off ...

One by one he also scratched out the others. Alex, a Greek haberdasher whose wife watched him so closely with her smouldering dark eyes that he couldn't have escaped her vigilance long enough to relieve himself behind a tree, let alone have an affair with Marian. Maylon, a liquor dealer, local Chamber of Commerce president and collector of pornography, whose interest in a female was known to end when she reached the age of sixteen. Britzlhoff, whose affair with Maylon's thin, strident wife had continued so long and so openly that it was no longer a subject for gossip. All these men, at one time or another, were thrown into proximity with Marian in the swirling crowd that filled the living room and spilled out on to the Japanese-lanterned terrace. As the party wore on and the liquor flowed, Carl Sanborn's eyes became unfocused, Britzlhoff disappeared with Maylon's wife, and the Greek goddess who was Alex's wife began to insist sullenly that it was time to leave. Dee ceased to notice who spoke to Marian. He became aware instead of one man who didn't: Joe Forrest.

Joe magnetized the females as Marian did the males.

Bailey's wife was a willowy blonde whose white gown sheathed her hips so tightly that the mound of her pelvis was thrown into sharp relief. She and Forrest had been the hottest affair on the lake during the previous summer; judging from the way her hands went out to touch him every time she spoke, it had ended through no fault of hers. There was also Gloria, a tiny dark-eyed girl not long out of her teens. A politician in Kansas City paid the rent for her three-story home across the cove. Between his visits to her, people going home in the small hours often saw Joe Forrest's Lincoln parked outside her house. And there was Betty Sanborn, whose husband would later be found sleeping peacefully in a bathtub or a clothes closet. She wore a green dress with the off-the-shoulder effect that gave her a look of partial undress, and tantalized the onlooker with the feeling that at any moment the gown would slip and expose the remaining half of her unbrassiered bosom. She was said to be the readiest woman at the lake; watching her, Dee could believe it. She moved her hips while she talked as though her rump were pressing against a hot steam pipe. While her mouth made polite conversation, her body moved in the convolutions of sex. Dee knew for certain that she had been Joe Forrest's mistress two years ago. Betty had admitted as much when she had asked Dee about the possibility of divorcing her husband. A week later she had told him bitterly to forget it, and Dee assumed that Joe Forrest had squelched the idea.

Dee looked at Joe's smooth handsomeness, the easy smile, the careless grace of gesture. Yes, it would be good for a man's ego to stand and talk to three women who had given themselves to him in the past and ached to do it again. He wondered how Joe felt about the husbands who nourished the sleek female flesh he enjoyed, who went on buying them furs and new cars, and let them drone away their summers in this lakeside Gomorrah. These husbands never knew that their wives peeled off their rich clothing for Joe Forrest, let him handle the well-fed flesh, and gave him access to the secret portal for which they, the husbands, paid so dearly.

And another question wriggled into his mind, who was Joe's latest interest? It was a shock for Dee to realize that he had no idea. He hadn't heard Joe's name mentioned for two weeks. Damn! Didn't that mean something? Wasn't the husband always the last to know?

He stood up so suddenly that the vodka martinis hit him like a whiff of ether. He staggered back, grabbed the chair, and caught his balance. *Jesus, didn't know I'd drunk so much. Gotta be careful, be cool, talk around the subject with someone else, be sure of my ground...*

He picked Betty Sanborn on the theory that a spurned mistress would know who currently enjoyed the favor of her ex-lover. He took her empty glass and told her she needed a refill. She was bleary and loose-limbed, and he had to support her all the way to the long table that held the liquor. When they got there, he said:

"Look, I was just kidding. You don't need another drink."

"The hell I don't. I gotta get drunk. How do I do that without drinking? Look at that."

Dee turned and saw that her husband had reached the fag-imitation stage of inebriation. There's one at every party, thought Dee. Carl was folding a napkin in such a way that when he held it up to his chest he seemed to have two white pointed breasts. He looked around at his smiling audience and then broke up into hiccupping giggles.

"See what I mean?" said Betty's voice in his ear. "He'll be drunk as a hog in a mudhole by the time we get home. And by God, so will I."

She turned back to the table and poured her glass half-full of vodka, dropped in an ice cube and drank deeply. "You know why I'm fuddling myself?" She looked at him, her mouth still wet. "Because he gets the idea he's Don Juan, Superman and Romeo all rolled into one. He's the great American lover when he's loaded. And half the time he goes to sleep in the saddle. Have you ever had that happen? I mean, have you got any idea what that does to a woman's pride?"

Dee lifted several shakers and sniffed them until he found one that held vodka martinis. One more wouldn't hurt him. He filled his glass and looked at

Betty; it seemed a good time to bring up Joe Forrest.

"Yes," he said. "I can't blame you for Joe."

"Joe." She said it flatly, and her face tightened up. "It's over. Kaput." She tilted up her glass, drained it, and gave Dee a sullen look. "You know that, Dee. Why the hell do you think I'm still with Carl?"

He managed a frown, then nodded. "I remember now. Who's his latest?"

She shrugged. "Who the hell knows? When a woman's ready, he knows it. Maybe they look different around the face. Maybe they give off an odor. I don't know how Joe knows, but he does. And when they're ready, he's there, eager to serve."

She laughed without mirth and leaned over to refill her glass. The dress lost its tenuous hold on her arm and fell below her elbow, the front slipping to reveal the crinkled half-moon of one nipple.

"Your dress is dripping," he said.

She looked up at him and smiled. There was nobody else at the liquor table, and their backs were to the crowd. "Would you like to adjust it?"

He smiled at her and shook his head.

"It's simple," she said. "Look." She straightened and caught the top of the dress in her hands. Instead of pulling upward, she pulled the cloth outward, away from her bosom. He saw the fullness of her breasts, the crinkled cups, the network of blue veins beneath the white skin, and the swollen convexity below.

"Dee?" She looked at him appealingly.

"Put them away," he said.

"All right. But let's take a little walk, huh?" She was adjusting the dress, at the same time moving closer and pressing the length of her thigh against him. "Take me out for some air."

"Look, Betty, you're a friend of Marian's—"

"So it would be just between friends, Dee. What do

you say?"

"No."

Her lips quirked. "You love your wife, huh?"

"Is that a crime?"

"No. But it's no goddamn virtue, either. Carl says he loves me, but that doesn't put lead in his pencil. Look at him." Dee glanced over his shoulder and saw that Carl had a strip of crepe tossed around his neck like a feather boa. He was mincing around with his hands on his hips.

"You think that's an act? Like hell it is. I'm his front. I'm a façade, just like those goddamn dirty jokes he tells. I make the bastard respectable so he can hang around his swishy friends without being suspected. I— oh, hell, Dee, I need it." Her fingers dug into his arm. "Take me out and give it to me. We'll be back before your wife is."

"My wife—?" He turned and saw that Marian was missing from the crowd. To Betty he said, "Where'd she go?"

"I don't know. The can, maybe. Dee, please—" She stretched out her hand and her dress slipped again. Dee did not look this time. He had just noticed that Joe Forrest was no longer in the room. He pulled away from Betty and walked toward the terrace, feeling a strange, buzzing sensation in his head.

They were not on the terrace. Dee felt a hard knot of anger clutch at his stomach; he stood still a moment and tried to control it, clenching his fists until his knuckles cracked. Keep calm, he told himself. Don't blow up at the party and maybe there'll be a few people who won't know that Joe Forrest is making out with your wife...

Dee walked back into the house. Betty grabbed him, murmuring that she was willing to forgive him for walking out on her, provided—

Dee interrupted as a new suspicion flashed through his mind. "Did you and Marian get everything settled this morning?"

She frowned, annoyed at the change of subject. "Settled?"

"Whatever you discussed on the phone."

She shook her head in bewilderment "I didn't call her this morning."

He felt the skin draw tight across his cheekbones. "Are you sure? She mentioned your name."

"Not mine. Betty's are a drug on the market. Thousands in existence."

"Not here at the lake." He turned and started away.

"Wait, Dee," Betty's face had suddenly become wary and alert. "I was thinking... I called a lot of people, maybe I called Marian. I think... yes, I remember now, we talked for several minutes..."

"At eleven?"

"Why... yes. Around there. Eleven or so."

"Thanks, Betty." He walked away. She had lied; the call had come through before ten. Never try to snow the old prosecutor, he said to himself, feeling a total absence of professional pride. He would rather not have known.

He found Joe and Marian five minutes later, standing on Carol's wooden dock. For a moment Dee paused at the top of the steps leading down to the dock, trying to still the pounding of blood in his temples, forcing down an urge to seize Joe's throat in his hands and squeeze until there was no life left in him. They were leaning against the railing and looking out over the water, standing at least a foot apart. They could have been a pair of casual acquaintances who had just happened to leave the party at the same time for a breath of air. Dee wished he could believe that; it would be such a wonderful thing to believe. And so damned impossible...

He walked softly down the steps. "Are the mosquitos bad tonight?" he asked casually, glad that his voice was light and airy.

Marian turned quickly, Joe more slowly, pulling a cigarette case from his pocket as he turned. "Not bad, Morgan. They sprayed last week."

"Joe was telling me," said Marian with only a hint of a quaver in her voice, "that some vandals have ruined his new cabin cruisers."

"Is that so?" Dee walked up and laid his hand on her shoulder. "Was he telling you that?" He squeezed slowly, applying an invisible pressure. "Or are you lying to me again?"

"Dee, what—?"

"I think I'll get back to the party," said Joe.

"You stay here," said Dee, feeling his anger rise. "Marian, go inside. Betty wants to see you."

"Dee, you've been drinking a lot. Maybe we'd better—"

"I said Betty wants to see you, dammit!" He drew in his breath slowly. "It's about the phone call she made to you this morning. You remember?"

Her lips opened in a soundless gasp, then clamped shut. She turned and he heard her heels clicking up wooden steps. He had a feeling she did not go all the way back to the house, but he did not bother to look.

Joe was offering him a cigarette. Dee ignored it. He was still proud of the way he held his temper.

"You handle yourself well, Forrest. You must have gone through this scene several times."

Joe knitted his brows. "Is this a riddle of some kind?"

"Someone's been fooling with my wife, Forrest."

Joe looked at the end of his cigarette. "That's a hard thing to say about your own wife."

Clenching his teeth, Dee said, "You let me worry about my wife, hear? You've got all the other wives to worry about."

"Morgan, I think you've had too much to drink. If you want to talk later..."

He started away, but Dee caught his arm and slammed him back against the railing. "Now!"

Joe went rigid, and for a second Dee thought the man was going to swing. Dee hoped he would; Forrest was at least twenty pounds lighter and three inches shorter, and Dee wasn't sure he could break a lifetime habit and attack a smaller man. He could strike the second blow, yes, but not the first...

To Dee's disappointment, Joe settled back against the rail and drew slowly on the cigarette. "All right, Morgan. I'm listening."

"Oh, I see we're going to be civilized, are we?" Dee tasted a sour frustration in his mouth. "It's nice to be civilized. So many men lose their heads in this kind of situation. I remember a case I had. A man pretended to go to work, then followed his wife to another man's house. He waited outside behind a shrub, drinking Sneaky Pete and making sure he had his shotgun loaded. When his wife came out he shot her in the neck with one barrel and tore her head off. The man got the other barrel in the stomach, down low. Took him eight hours to die. The killer got ten years in the pen; it was the most I could get out of the jury. Funny how they always sympathize with the husband."

"Look, Morgan, is there any point—?"

"I'm getting to it, Forrest. Relax."

Joe sighed and sagged against the railing. "Go on."

"Not everybody uses a gun, Joe. I had another case where the husband went to his wife with his evidence and scared her into helping him get revenge. The woman made a date with her lover, telling him that her husband would be out of town. But the husband wasn't. He was under the bed with a loop of strong, thin wire through a hole in the mattress. The woman's job was to arrange herself in bed so that the man would be in the right position. Then she fixed the loop in place and signaled her husband. He tightened the loop and jerked with all his strength. The wire worked like a razor blade and the man was left in a state which made him totally uninteresting to women. He cried to the cops. The husband got four years, the wife one."

Joe flipped his cigarette into the water. "That's a helluva story, Morgan. You have a reason for telling it?"

"Just to show you what a risky hobby you've got, Joe. If you turned up dead, there'd be so many men with motives that a clever man could lose himself in the crowd."

Joe looked at him narrowly. "You regard yourself as a clever man?"

"Clever enough. And I know about your hideaway back in the woods."

Joe stiffened, and Dee knew he'd surprised him. "One of your women had a foolish idea you were serious enough to marry her. She told me about the cabin. If my wife turns up missing, that's where I'll look for her. You understand?"

"You won't find your wife there."

"You deny that she was there last night?"

"You're damn right, I deny it."

"That you've ever asked her to come?"

"I deny that, too."

"You deny that you want her?"

"What am I supposed to say? She's a damned attractive woman. Unfortunately, she's happily married." Joe started to light another cigarette, then paused to look at Dee. "Maybe you'd better appreciate that. Not go around trying to dig up trouble. A woman with a jealous husband soon gets the feeling she might as well have the game as the name."

Dee had used up all his patience and gotten nowhere with Forrest. But there was still Marian.

"All right, Joe. You're cool. But I don't believe you. And I'll kill the man I find with my wife. Remember that."

Without waiting for an answer, he turned and trotted up the steps. He met Marian at the top, just starting down. He caught her arm and turned her around. "We're going home."

"All right, but—you're hurting my arm!"

He held on, half-dragging her across the green expanse of lawn that separated their house from Carol's. The noise of the party faded behind them.

"Who'd you call this morning?"

"Betty. She'd forgotten. She remembers now."

"Sure. You broads alibi each other."

She lost a high-heeled pump and stopped to pick it up. Dee jerked her arm. "Come on." She limped for several steps on one shoe, then jerked it off and walked on bare feet. Outside the door, she stopped.

"Dee, can't we talk?"

"Tell me where you were last night."

"I told you. In bed."

"Sure. Only the bed was in a little cabin in the woods with twin speakers on a hi-fi, and a little switch that turns on the coffee pot in the kitchen."

She had walked ahead of him into the living room. Now she turned, her face pale, but determined. "He lied if he said that."

"Who lied?"

"Joe. I wasn't in his cabin."

"How'd you know I described Joe's cabin?"

He would have thought it impossible for her face to go any paler, but it did. Her mouth dropped open and she stared at him without speaking. Then she caught her breath. "I've ... I've heard the girls ... you'd been talking to Joe ... I just assumed."

"You're lying." He felt rage rise up and choke him. He covered the space between them in a single stride and seized the front of her dress. "You were with him, weren't you? Admit it!"

She jumped backward, and the dress ripped apart beneath her arms. She kept backing away, her torn dress around her waist, her breasts jumping inside the half-cup of her brassiere.

"You—you have nothing but suspicion, Dee. You're spoiling everything for a silly, stupid suspicion."

Dee stayed where he was. "Maybe I can get proof. Carol had something on her mind when she came to see me last night."

"Carol?" Marian's eyes widened. "Carol went to see you last night at the hotel?"

"I told you—"

"Did she stay in your room?"

"She slept on the other bed," Dee said. He didn't like the latest turn of conversation. He was losing the initiative. "And I left soon after she got there."

"Are you trying to tell me this was a brother-sister scene?" Her lower lip curled. "Are you trying to tell me that my dear best friend would pass up a chance to get in bed with you? God! I'll bet she was pulling down her pants before she said hello."

"Marian, you're going off on a tangent."

"Oh, am I? Am I really? Well, you don't have to tell me what happened between you and Carol. She'll tell me. She'll be only too happy to."

Marian was probably right, thought Dee. "Carol wasn't important."

She looked at him incredulously. "Wasn't... Then you did?"

"I said it wasn't important."

"Oh, my God." Her lips trembled. "My best friend—my husband. And it wasn't important. And what..." She drew herself up and her eyes flashed fire. "And what the hell is important? If that isn't nothing is. Not even Joe Forrest. Right?"

"That's different."

"And how the hell is it different?"

"With a woman, it's different."

"Oh, please, I expected something less medieval. Why is it different? Because I just lay there and took it? Because I was for heaven's sake on the bottom? Because he was in me instead of the other way around? Where's the difference? You took a shower after Carol and became suddenly clean again. Pure and untarnished. So why can't I take a shower after Joe and become—"

She stopped and stared at him, her mouth half open. He heard the sound of laughter from the party next door, a crash of a glass breaking on the terrace. He felt a tightness in his skull.

"So you did go with him."

"Yes."

He felt a nausea in his stomach. Until she had said that, no matter how the proof stacked up, he could always hope in the back of his mind that she was innocent. Now the hope was dead. And he felt as though he were dead, too.

"What are you going to do?" she asked.

"Leave you," he said. "Get the hell away from you. I don't want to see you again."

"Dee. Dee, we're even now. Let's start over."

"Impossible."

"No, it isn't. Listen. You wanted me this morning, didn't you? Am I any different now? Look." She raised her hands to the brassiere and tore it off. She cupped her breasts in her palms and looked at him. "You said they were beautiful. Are they any different now?"

"Another man has handled them."

"And that changes them? No. Look." She pushed down the torn remnant of her dress and stepped out of it. The panties followed and she stood in her black garter belt and nylon stockings. "Now what do you see?"

He saw sweat-gleaming flesh, breasts trembling with the quickness of her breathing, garter belt framing womanhood like an archway over a little garden.

"Dee. Is it any different because someone else has used it?"

"Don't—" He tried to tell her not to mention that again because he didn't think he could control himself. But a lump had lodged in his throat and he couldn't talk.

She mistook his speechlessness for something else. She walked toward him. "Dee, I know you won't find this easy to believe, but I love you all the more. You liked me this morning. You said so—"

"I didn't know you'd just come from that bastard."

"But we hadn't done anything for—"

"Shut up!"

"—several hours—"

Something exploded in his brain and filled it with red fire. He did not realize he had hit her until he saw her sprawled on the floor, holding her hand to her jaw, looking at him with shocked horror. He thought, God, that's something I didn't intend to do.

He squatted beside her and lifted her head into his lap. "Marian, I didn't mean that. I had too much to drink, can't control—"

"Dee..." She moved her jaw and winced, "You aren't leaving?"

He clamped his teeth tightly. "Yes, I am. I couldn't

stand to look at you—"

She closed her eyes. "Dee... telephone..."

He became aware of the insistent ringing. He picked up the receiver and held it to his ear. "Morgan speaking."

"This is long distance. Just a moment."

He waited, watching Marian get up and start picking up her clothes. Her shoulders slumped, her breasts sagged; she looked very tired.

Dee heard an urgent voice in his ear. "Mr. Morgan? Mr. Morgan?"

"Speaking. Who—?"

"This is Bill Fisher, director of the Walnut Ridge Youth Camp. Could you come right away? Your daughter—"

"Sharon?" A cold chill climbed his spine. "What's happened?"

"She's not hurt, Mr. Morgan. I mean, physically she's perfectly all right. But she wants to see you right away. She's... very upset. Hysterical—"

"Do you have any idea why?"

"It's something to do with a new boy who came to camp this morning, but she refuses to tell anybody but you."

"Me? What about her mother?"

"No. She's emphatic on that. She wants to see only you."

"Doesn't she want to see her mother?"

"Definitely not."

"All right. I'll be there. Two or three hours."

He hung up, frowning. He turned to look at Marian. She was sitting in a chair with her clothes on her lap, as though her strength had suddenly given way. She stared at him, eyes wide, nostrils pinched and white. Her look was that of someone who had been hit on the head with a rock.

"You heard what I was saying," Dee growled. "You have any idea why she doesn't want to see you?"

She shook her head slowly from side to side, then lowered her eyes and fingered the clothes in her lap.

"You're lying," said Dee. "But I'll get the truth from Sharon."

He went to the bathroom and swallowed a Dexamyl capsule to help him stay awake. Marian did not look up as he walked across the room and went out the door. He was getting into his car when Carol ran up.

"Dee, what's wrong? You disappeared from the party—"

"It's too long a story to tell now. I'm going to see Sharon. Stay with Marian, and this time don't let her out of your sight."

He drove off without looking back. The Dexamyl made him feel strong and confident. He could handle Sharon's trouble, whatever it was. A twelve-year-old's problems couldn't be much, compared to his own.

8

Lewis dumped the last bundle of loot in his boat and stepped back to assess his load. Two carpets, a coil of rope, two air mattresses, a Coleman lantern, a camp stove, an ax, a skillet, a pan, table setting for two, a large cardboard crate full of canned food. Four cabins along the lake, their owners absent, had yielded him enough provisions to last two weeks.

As he steered his boat toward the opposite, uninhabited shore, Lewis felt exultant. How easy it was, he thought, when a man had a plan. And how quickly everything fell into place, little bits of knowledge he had picked up before he had even dreamed of kidnaping a woman. First, he had remembered those vacant cabins, then he had recalled the cave he had stumbled on three months before. It had taken him most of the day to find the brush-choked ravine which led to the cave, but that was good. Nobody else could find it by accident. He would have at least two weeks alone with Marian and after that—

What happened after that would depend on how well she pleased him.

He aimed his boat toward the rocky headland which was his landmark, deflected his course into the little cove, and beached his boat. Three trips were necessary to transport his load up the ridge and down into the ravine, and pile it outside the crab apple thicket which protected the entrance to the cave. He took his ski-rope from the boat, tied the bundle inside one of the blankets, and lowered it down the black hole. It was ten feet to the floor of the cavern. When he felt the bundle touch bottom, he tied one end of the rope to a tree and lowered himself hand over hand. It was like sinking into a pool of black ink. He fumbled inside the bundle, found his flashlight and propped it on a rock. By its beam, Lewis unpacked the lantern. He filled the spirit cup, lit up, and watched the blue flame suffuse the mantle. He squatted on his heels and waited for it to generate. He was a patient man. One had to be patient when stalking that greatest game of all—woman.

As he watched, the mantle began to resemble a white, oval face. Swirling flames supplied the hair, and those two charred spots in the fabric were eyes. He saw the shadow of the nose, the shape of the mouth. Marian. She was smiling at him; no, the mouth was changing, now she was screaming at him, and her eyes were going wide with fear. For a second he could hear her voice coming out of the spirit flame:

Lewis, don't kill me. I love you, Lewis...

He felt the hard, hot excitement in his groin. He watched the flame and waited to see what she would do next. It was changing; now the face belonged to someone else. Marge. The tendrils of smoke swirled across the mantle like her hair, loose and floating in deep water, waving gently over her face. A red blotch appeared on her forehead and spread downward. Her blood, thick and black, poured from the wound, and her eyes turned toward him, accusing ....

"No! Get out!"

He lurched forward to turn off the lamp and end the vision. As her finger touched the knob, he stopped. A new face was forming, a very young face, with red hair and a sprinkle of bright freckles across her turned-up nose. It was a face he had seen before—but where? He leaned closer and peered into the spirit flame, trying to remember ...

He gasped as though he had been hit in the stomach. *Dolores.* The first one. My God, how many years? I was fifteen then and she was—yes, she was two grades behind me and that made her thirteen ...

In a moment it all came back to him, the smell of the dusty grass beside the path, the star-bursts of spattered cow-dung in the thick dust, the thick, humid air and the sun like a white-hot rivet in the pale sky. Three of them went swimming with Lewis that day: Dolores and her two brothers. Fred was also fifteen and Bobby was only ten. The pond belonged to Lewis' grandfather—an oval sink of muddy water choked at one end by a clump of cattails, buzzing with four-winged snake-feeders, and bordered by a dike of mud pushed up by the hoofs of drinking cattle. Fred and Bobby ran the last forty yards shouting, "Last one in is a jackass!" They unhooked the suspenders of their Lee overalls as they ran, dropped them on the weed-grown dam, stood for a moment in their white shorts, then disappeared over the side in a flash of brown backs crisscrossed by white suspender-marks. Lewis walked slowly beside Dolores, not wanting to appear undignified and callow in her eyes. He was totally in love with her, but she had slapped him once when he had tried to kiss her, and had threatened once to tell her mother when he tried to put his hand up her dress on the school bus. But Lewis hadn't given up.

When they reached the pond, Lewis walked behind the cattails and dropped his overalls. He waded in and felt thick mud grip his ankles. He saw Dolores seat herself on the bank and pull the flowered cotton dress over her knees.

"Aren't you coming in?" asked Lewis.

She wrinkled her turned-up nose. "The water stinks."

Lewis agreed, but Fred laughed. "That ain't the reason, Lew. She ain't suppose to show herself because—"

"Fred, you shut up!"

"—She got two bumblebee stings on the—"

"Fred, I'll tell!"

"—tits and that ain't all she's got—"

Splat! A gob of smelly mud struck Fred's shoulder. He dashed for the bank, splashing like a water-buffalo and shouting: "Damn you! I'll give you a taste of mud—!"

Lewis stood frozen in the knee-deep water and watched Fred chase his sister across the dam, seize her around the waist, and carry her kicking and clawing to the water's edge. He should help her, he knew that. But the talk of her body had started a licking flame inside him. Fred's struggle with her excited him even more. He watched Fred hook his heel behind her legs and push her backward into the muddy pond. Splash! She floundered, then rose, sobbing. The dress was plastered against tight little buttocks and revealed clearly the line of her panties. She splashed out of the water, ran up the bank, then turned and shouted:

"Fred, you just wait till the folks get home! You'll get your hide peeled!"

At first the words didn't register with Lewis. He was too busy observing how the wet dress molded the front of her body. Bigger than bee-stings, he thought, more like little teacups set wide apart on her chest. The dress clung to her little belly and strong muscular thighs, making her look almost naked. Lewis felt the skin draw tight on his scalp. A hot lump rose up in his throat as she whirled and ran off through the ragwood, toward her house a half-mile away. Lewis turned to Fred, and his voice sounded strange in his ears.

"Where's your folks, Fred?"

"Landon. Mom hadda see the doctor." He kneeled and started washing off the mud. "They ain't gonna be home till dark. She'll forget about it by then." He pushed off and started swimming across the pond. "Hell with her. It's more fun without her."

Lewis didn't agree. He told the others he had to go home and water the sows, then put on his overalls and left. His heart was pounding when he reached the deep gully just below the pond. He ran along the dry sandy bottom, climbed the water-gap dividing his grandfather's land from that of Dolores' parents, and ran on. He left the cover of the gully and plunged into a cockle-burr patch that hid him until he reached the garden. Then he crawled on his hands and knees between rows of sweetcorn reaching practically to the kitchen door. He knew where her room was. He pounded silently up the stairs and ran inside. Across one corner was a curtain behind which she hung her clothes. He parted the curtain, squatted down behind the skimpy collection of dresses, and waited. His heart began to thump painfully against his chest, and his breathing turned hoarse and ragged. *Jesus, she'll hear that, gotta control it.*

He heard the wheeze of the kitchen pump, then silence. His hands began shaking; his mind swirled with a vision of her taking off the muddy clothes, standing naked in a dishpan, washing herself. And they were alone in the house. He could tiptoe down and just take a look. He tried to rise, but his knees buckled and he sat down again.

Bare feet slapped on the stairway. The door opened. He smelled wet flesh, heard the sound of her voice humming a tune. Trembling, he leaned forward and peered through the narrow opening in the curtain. She was standing in front of her mirror and toweling herself. *Oh, God, there she is, all of her, wet and shiny. Funny the way they start out real sudden from her chest, then sorta round off into little rose-colored knobs. She's covering them with the towel, rubbing them hard, looking sideways at herself in the mirror. Oh, please, let me do that for you ... Now drying her stomach, legs, bending her knees and turning around to face me ... Oh, God ...*

He could not remember exactly what happened after he leaped through the curtain. He heard a sharp, piercing scream, so loud it frightened him. All he thought about then was that somebody would hear. Fear made him strong, and he seized her naked, twisting body and said, "Please be quiet. Please, I won't hurt you. Please, please—!"

"Fred—Bobby—Help!"

He tried to stop her voice with his hand but she sank her teeth into his palm. Now he had pain to accompany his fear, and gradually the two feelings joined into a rage which drowned his mind in fire. "Shut up," he said. "Shut up shut up shut up shut up shut up shut up—"

He was still saying it when he wrapped the towel around her neck and twisted it with all his strength. He had only one thought: to choke off the air that fed her screeching voice. He still was saying it when he realized she was no longer fighting him, and she lay limp beneath him...

He let go of the towel and leaned back on his haunches, gasping for breath. "Now ... you'll be quiet ... won't you?"

She did not answer. She lay with her face toward the ceiling, her eyes half-closed as though heavy with sleep. He heard the buzzing of a fly so loud it seemed to be buzzing inside his head. He watched it light on her cheek and begin crawling; it crawled over her open eye and she didn't move.

Oh, God. I've killed her.

Slowly the horror crept over him. He stared at her without moving. He looked at her and felt a hot wave of grief spread through his chest.

He lay his hand on her thigh. She felt different. Her skin wasn't cold, it was just ... what? There was no sense of life beneath her skin. All movement had stopped within her: the thump of her heart, the racing currents of blood through her veins, the gurgle of her stomach and the twitch of her nerves. Now there was no thrill in touching, no thrill even in looking ...

Fear washed over him in an icy bath. *They'll kill me. Got to do something ...*

He jumped up and ran to the window. Fred and Bobby were coming across the pasture; they had willow switches which they used like sabers, slashing off the tops of ragweed. They were only a couple of hundred yards away; he had to work fast. He looked around quickly and saw the square opening in the ceiling which led to the attic. He pushed a chair under it and strained to force the girl's body through the hole. On the first try, she slid back, fell to his shoulders, and then made a sodden, sickening thump on the floor. On the second try, he got her in and pulled himself behind her into the choking oven of the attic. Sweat drenched him as he pulled her away from the entry. He had seen dead livestock after only a few hours in the heat. He knew he had no more than a day before she would advertise her presence; he had to move fast, get far out of the country before they caught him ...

He ran silently out through the kitchen, back the way he had come. On the highway, he caught a cattle truck which carried him to a town forty miles away. In the stockyards, he hitched a grain semi west to Kansas, then snagged a freight to Denver. For two days he milked cows for an old lady there. She thought he was sweet, but he took fifty dollars from her purse and hit out for California. Picking fruit. Pitching hay. Milking cows.

He began to feel safe, but he dared not touch a woman for two years. Not until that time he found the girl sleeping in the park in Ventura. Later he was bumming through Salt Lake City, flat broke, and a chubby waitress sneaked him into her boarding house. She let him sleep with her, after he promised to leave his pants on and be a gentleman. When he forgot his promise later, she fought silently, with nails and teeth; until he opened his knife and pushed the point through her panty-girdle, just pricking her buttock. She lay stiff with fright until near the end. When Lewis felt her fingers digging into his back and heard the low meaningless sounds in her throat, he discovered something about women: *Some fight when they don't really want to.*

And so he had gone on taking the women as they came, making love to those who wanted it, ignoring the struggles of those who thought they had to fight, and raping those who seemed to invite it. But he had never killed another one, not until ... *what was her name? Marge. Damn, my memory faded away there, took a little tour through the past. Can't waste time, gotta get Marian's new home ready for her ...*

The spirit cup was nearly empty. Lewis turned up the valve and the mantle glowed white, filling the cave with light. Lewis lifted the lantern and looked around. The cave was about the width and height of a box car, but only half as long. Horizontal channels in the limestone walls showed that it had been scoured out by an underground river. What remained of the river trickled down one end, flowed along the right-hand wall to disappear into a pool on the other side. He dipped his hand in the pool and tasted it: cold and sweet. No trouble about water. The gods were on his side ...

He set the lantern on a shoulder-high shelf of limestone, then started clearing a section of the floor. Loose rock, a few ancient, mouldy leaves, and three rabbit skeletons. The skeletons told him there was no way out except through the roof. He would be able to pull up the rope and leave Marian for hours at a time.

He spread out the rugs, set up the camp stove, and started putting the canned goods on the limestone. He had brought mostly heat-and-serve foods: chow mein dinners, franks and beans, ravioli in sauce, pork and beans, corned beef, soups, canned stew, and so forth.

Lewis blew up the air-mattresses, lay them side by side, covered them with blankets. He stretched out on his back and tried the bed for comfort. He didn't like being this close to the ground; maybe later he would take his ax and make a platform to sleep on. A big wide one, so there would be no need to have her lying against him when he was through with her for the night.

He lay with his hands behind his head, looking at the inky shadows on the wall. He imagined Marian with him, moving softly about the cave so she would not disturb him. There she was at the camp stove, stirring the beans, brushing the golden hair from her eyes. Dressed? Yes, wearing shorts and the red halter which swung so delightfully when she bent over. He would make her wear clothes, so he could watch her take them off when he gave the word.

Now she was bathing in the little pool, dipping cups of water and pouring them on the back of her neck; funny how the water formed a pattern down her back and between her breasts, disappearing for a moment, then runing down the inside of her legs ... Now she stood before him, her eyes pleading. *I want to see the sun,* said her lips. *I'll do whatever you want, but I want to see the sun.* He smiled sleepily. *Dance for me.* So she danced, moving her white body in a sensuous rhythm, watching his face with a wariness which made him feel powerful. *Faster,* he said. *And hotter.* She began to move her hips in circles, her arms in front of her as though she held some invisible man against her. She ran her hands up her body, over her breasts to her face, pulling the hair down over her eyes until it waved gently, as though everything were under water. But look—it was the wrong girl.

"Marge, get out!" yelled Lewis. The dead girl disappeared, leaving a shadowed niche in the wall which resembled no woman at all. To the wall he said, "Marian, come back." And there she was, taking shape, only... why was the towel around her neck? And the hair was wrong, shouldn't be red, oh, no ... not her, with the open eyes, the tender body, not Dolores ...

He tried to push away the vision, but Dolores

remained. And she was changing. Her body was growing larger, but no, not really growing, merely puffing out as the heat in the attic took its effect. And now the skin was peeling, flesh sloughing off, and there was nothing left but a skeleton. That's all she was, just bones, bones ...

He got up and wiped the cold sweat from his face. What did it mean? Had the family gone away and never found her body? Had she just laid up there and rotted? He had wondered about it many times, and each time he had had to chop off the thought and work puzzles in his head, anything to push his mind away from Dolores ...

He had to get out of the cave. It was no good alone, too full of visions. He looked at his watch. Two a.m. Time he thought, to get Marian.

He shoved gun and flashlight into his pocket, hung binoculars around his neck, before climbing the rope. He lay a dead branch over the hole, pulled up and untied the rope. He walked back to his boat, rowed out into the main channel before starting the motor, just in case someone was near.

The journey to the cove took him past Mac's Pizza Palace. He stayed in the main channel, cut his engine, and raised the binoculars. They were 7x50's with coated lenses, and they drew enough light to let him see better than with the naked eye. Yes, there was that twitch-butted high-school girl with those new-sprouting little breasts you could probably shape to suit yourself as she grew up. Had a kind of date with her tonight, didn't he? And there was a chance, just from the way she swung her butt, that ...

He set his teeth against the fiery desire in him, started the motor. He headed for the cove where he always left the boat. This time he covered it carefully with branches; it was his last visit and he couldn't afford to be spotted.

On top of the ridge, he paused, and lifted the glasses. His heart leaped when he saw that Dee's car was gone. There was a light in the house. Somebody was home. Not Dee, so it had to be Marian. Now, if she were alone...

He walked silently to the edge of the bank that rose above the driveway. He sat down in the shadow of a gooseberry bush and peered through the glasses. The bedrooms were visible, but the living room was on the other side of the house, facing the lake. Nightlight burning in Marian's bedroom; nobody in bed. Husband's room on left, dark. Bathroom lit, door opening—

Son of a bitch! That damned skinny woman, that girlfriend, Carol. What was she doing here—sentry duty? He watched her fumble in the medicine cabinet, take out a bottle, probably aspirin—swallow two pills, then walk back toward the door. As she opened the door, he saw Marian seated on the sofa with her housecoat belted tightly around her. She was holding her chin in her hands, looking miserable.

The door closed, and Lewis rose. He had taken one step when he heard a shriek of laughter from the house next door. Hell. A party, terrace full of people, fights, damn cars parked all along the drive, the glow of cigarettes under trees. Something white flashed on the dock. Splash! Hell, that broad was either naked or she wore a transparent swimsuit...

Well, he couldn't go down now, couldn't fight all those people. He looked at his watch. Almost three. He would wait until the party ended, or until everybody passed out. One or the other usually happened by daylight. By then Carol would have gone back to her own house, and Marian would be alone.

If not ... well, hell. He felt the weight of the gun in

his pocket. Nobody would stop him, even if he had to kill again. He had nothing to lose, and a woman to gain...

He went back to the top of the ridge to wait.

9

Marian drew her feet up on the couch and glared at Carol, infuriated by the sedate expression on the woman's face as she turned the pages of her book. Marian knew there would be no sleep for her tonight; not after that scene with Dee—*oh, God, that horrible, horrible scene!* Now her nerves were drawn into knots as she waited for the telephone to ring. Sharon must have heard about what those boys had seen on the ridge. Nothing else would throw the girl into hysterics. Soon Dee would call and ...

Or would he call? Maybe he would simply send one of those stiff, formal letters, something like: ... *and so I hope for the sake of our daughter we can avoid a public spectacle in court. You are welcome to any property settlement you desire, of course. Sharon stays with me—*

Marian groaned.

No ... no ... Oh, Lord, I don't want to lose her too ...

Carol raised her head. "What did you say?"

"Nothing."

"Yes, you said something about—"

"I said nothing!" Marian clenched her fists and brought

her voice under control. "Why don't you go back to your party?"

"Will you come with me?"

Marian poured a drink from the half-empty bourbon bottle. It had been full an hour ago. "I'm fine right here."

Carol shrugged and turned back to her book. "Well, I can't leave you alone. Not the way you're boozing."

Marian glared, wondering what would happen if she ordered the other woman out of the house. Carol would probably ignore her. Anyway, Marian wasn't sure she wanted the other woman to leave. It would be sheer hell to sit alone with her thoughts; even worse than being at the party around people she did not know very well. Carol didn't matter; Carol was like one of the family—

The thought made her sit up. *One of the family.* My God, how apt that was. Dee's other wife, Dee's bedmate, Dee's home away from home. Marian had not told Carol that she knew about the affair with Dee last night. One reason Marian had not brought up the subject was that she was not sure how she felt about it. Angry, of course. But a curiously diffused anger directed in equal parts at Dee, Carol and herself. Mostly at herself. Lord, she had known for fifteen years that Carol would throw a scissor-hold on Dee the moment she got a chance. And Marian blamed herself for having given Carol the chance. Marian had neglected to keep the home fires burning, so Dee had gone next door to get warm. Could she blame him for that?

Damn right I can, she said to herself. Both of them, getting together behind my back, sneaking off to the city ...

In a sudden flash of mental clarity, she realized that was what she hated most: being left out. Like when two people have a secret they won't tell you. Like having to stay at home while the rest of the kids went to the game. Like being cheated ...

She looked at Carol and suddenly understood the peaceful look on her face. Had Dee been so good for her? Had that big, awkward husband of hers given the woman so much joy that it still shone from her face? Marian felt a surge of envy, then curiosity. What had he done with Carol that he had never done with his wife? Oh—nonsense! For Carol, it had just been the thrill of something new.

She thought of Joe, remembering the shock when his hands had touched her intimately. He had a different manner, smoother than Dee's. Slower too, so that her body, geared to Dee's sudden, rough assault, had writhed impatiently as she had waited for Joe. It had been good, yes; Joe seemed more concerned for her pleasure than his own. Yet there had been an awkwardness which had left her with a faint aftertaste of frustration...

You have to learn the other's way. Where had she heard that? Oh, God. Lewis. She shuddered and drew her housecoat around her. For a second she could feel those strange, fixed eyes on her, watching her. But that was impossible. Lewis had left the country; Joe had been telling her that tonight when Dee had interrupted.

A crash came from Carol's house, then a burst of laughter.

"They'll pull it down to the foundations," said Marian.

"It's insured," said Carol, without looking up.

"You're a lousy hostess."

Carol shrugged again. "So are you."

Marian poured another drink, ignoring Carol's raised eyebrow. The alcohol was bringing a lightness to Marian's head, but it wasn't enough yet. She could still visualize, with horrible clarity, the scene that must take place, or was now taking place, between Sharon and Dee. How had Sharon found out? Of course, those boys would have talked, and the story would have spread until every child in the area between ten and seventeen had come to know that Mrs. Morgan was on the ridge naked with a man. Or would it be four men? Would they exaggerate? No, the truth was bad enough. And Sharon would have overheard, or would have been told by a friend in a moment of spite.

And Sharon would hate her. She had a teenager's black-white conception of morality. A thing was good, or it was bad. There were no extenuating circumstances, not even for a mother ...

Marian felt tears of self-pity burn her eyelids.

Not wanting Carol to see, Marian rose and went into the bathroom. She regarded her face in the mirror and ran her hand over her swollen jaw. It was sore, but there was no permanent damage. God, she thought, I wish he had knocked me down on the floor and cracked my ribs, broken an arm, closed an eye. Maybe if my body was racked with pain I wouldn't feel so bad in my mind—

She felt a hand on her shoulder. Carol stood behind her, looking at her in the mirror. "Does it hurt?"

"Only when I laugh."

"Why did he hit you?"

Marian was about to tell Carol to mind her own business, then realized she was aching to talk.

"We had a fight about Joe Forrest."

"Because Dee saw you talking to him?"

"Not only that. He found out I ... I..."

Marian could not finish her confession, but Carol supplied the words. "You went to his cabin last night."

Marian whirled. "How do you know?"

"I followed you."

"You—?"

"Listen to the rest of it. I followed you, then I took off for the city. I was going to tell Dee. I was going to edge you out and take your place. I'd been waiting for a chance to kick apart your marriage and this was it. So I went in and ..." She shrugged. "I couldn't do it."

"Why?"

"He'd be no damn good to me, Marian. He'd be no good to anybody without you—"

"Oh, Carol—"

"It's true. You've got him. Maybe you don't appreciate that, but you've got all there is that's good of him."

Marian looked at her narrowly. "You looked happy a few minutes ago. Now you don't."

"It comes—and goes." Carol started to smile wryly, but instead shiny tears appeared in her eyes. Marian suddenly forgot her own problems.

"Come on," she said, seizing the tall girl's arm. "Let's have a drink."

She poured the bourbon straight, a double shot apiece. Carol drained hers in two swallows and set the glass on the coffee table with a click. "More."

Marian poured. "You'll get drunk."

"I couldn't think of a better time. Join me?"

Marian lifted her glass and looked across it. She heard a swarm of bees buzzing inside her head but she didn't care. "All right. Bottoms up."

"To your marriage."

The bourbon burned Marian's throat but the pain was a friend. It made her forget the other ache. She set down her empty glass. "No use drinking to my marriage. Dee's ending it."

"He's just saying that."

"No. He means it." She felt the sadness well up again, and drank from the glass Carol had filled for her. A looseness came into her bones and she slumped on the couch, holding her glass in her lap.

"He will mean it after tonight," she said glumly. "There was more than Joe."

"More than—" Carol gasped. "My God, sedate, little

Marian. I would never have dreamed—" She filled her glass, kicked off her shoes, and unbuttoned the neck of her green cocktail dress. She leaned back on the couch, tucked her feet beneath her, and said, "All right, I want to hear all about it."

Marian told the story of Lewis, their meeting on the ridge, the discovery, then his attempt to break in which had led her to call Joe for help. When she finished, the envy had left Carol's face and in its place was a look of sympathy. One bottle had been emptied and another begun. Marian was crying maudlin tears.

Carol slid an arm across her shoulders.

"Marian, if I ever saw a woman get screwed up by circumstances, that's you. Didn't you tell Dee any of this?"

"No."

"You should have. Right at the beginning."

"Yes, but—God! I told one lie, and then I had to tell another to back it up. And I kept getting in deeper and deeper."

"Tell him when he gets back," she said. "It will help."

"It won't." Marian reached for her drink and tipped it over. She fumbled to pick it up but the table shimmered and she lurched forward. Carol caught her and pulled her back.

"You're drunk," said Carol. "Here." She filled the glass and held it to Marian's lips.

"So'r you," said Marian, drinking.

"I can hold more'n you. Always could."

Marian giggled. "What about the time you passed out at the dance. In the car. I went out and the parking attendant had you almost undressed—"

"Bastard. Lucky thing you came before he got too far. Here. Drink again."

Time passed, and the room swirled. Still the phone was silent, but Marian was not looking at it so often.

"Did I tell you about Lewis?" asked Marian. "Hey, I did. Confessed all. Opened my heart. Right?"

Carol nodded.

"So okay, do the same for me," Marian urged.

"What'll I confess?"

"Dee and you. Last night. Separate beds, he tried to tell me at first."

Carol focused her eyes blearily and for a moment seemed sober. "At first? What about later?"

"Later he admitted it."

"You're not angry?"

"I don't know. Haven't decided."

"Well, look, I ..." Carol seemed about to apologize, then changed her mind. "What else did he say?"

Marian smiled tauntingly over her glass. "Wouldn't you like to know?"

"Marian, please—"

"He said it wasn't important."

Carol's face seemed to shrink, and Marian was sorry she had spoken. She hadn't meant to hurt Carol.

"Carol, he didn't say that—"

"Yes. Yes, he did. And I guess he's right. It wasn't important to him."

Marian watched a tear slide down the inner side of Carol's nose and drop off the end. She could not hate Carol, a girl she had known so many years. She slid her arm around Carol's waist and put her head on her shoulder. "Look, I'm not sore. If it had to be someone, I'm glad it was you."

"It won't happen again," said Carol, her voice desolate. "I can't compete with what you've got." She turned to look at Marian, and her eyes were strangely bright. "I always wanted what you had, you know that? I used to watch you when we roomed together, in the bathroom, taking a shower, changing clothes. And I used to wonder about myself."

Marian stared at her, bewildered by the sudden change in Carol. "Wonder? Why?"

"Because of what I felt like doing."

It was more than the liquor, Marian thought, which caused the sudden giddiness in her head. "That was so long ago—"

"But you haven't changed. And neither have I."

Marian gasped as Carol loosened the belt of her robe, then threw it open. Marian knew she should stop the woman, hold the hand which moved so gently across her stomach, enclosing her breast. But a strange weakness weighed her body. She sank back on the couch and said weakly. "Carol, what's wrong with you?"

"Drunk maybe. I don't realize what I'm doing."

Marian felt the hand caress her leg, then the touch of lips on her breast, on her stomach. Marian stretched out her hand and dug her fingers into Carol's hair. "The lights ..."

"You want them off?"

"If you're going to—" She caught herself; there was no question but that Carol was going through with it. And Marian wanted her to. "Yes. Turn them off."

Carol rose, carefully walked to the end of the couch, and turned off the lamp. Next she walked across the room. She turned off the kitchen light. A faint light came through the window from Carol's terrace. Marian watched Carol come toward her, a dim shape in the darkness. The woman paused in front of the couch, and Marian heard the quick snick of the zipper, then the rustling noise as Carol pulled the dress over her head and threw it on the floor. Two more quick movements and Carol stood nude before her. The sight of Carol's pointed breasts gave her a sudden feeling of panic. *My God, this is a woman. What am I doing?*

"Carol, have you ever before—?"

"No."

"Then how do you know what—?"

"How did Adam know?" Marian felt Carol's hand on her knee. The tall slim shape folded itself on the couch beside Marian. She felt the palms slide up and down her legs. She pressed her shoulders back against the couch and slid herself forward, saying without conviction:

"Carol, we shouldn't."

"In the morning we'll say we were drunk."

Marian giggled crazily. "It's almost morning now."

"Shhh! Relax."

Marian felt the gentle pressure of the palms forcing her knees apart. She lay her head back and closed her eyes, giving herself up to Carol. There was nothing for Marian to do but let it happen. It was something totally new, totally different ...

It was full daylight when Marian rose from the couch. Pink light came through the windows. Carol hadn't bothered to go home for a change, but had borrowed an extra housecoat of Marian's. Now she was in the kitchen, making coffee. Marian decided she looked drawn and haggard. Purple shadows lay under her eyes. *We'll say we were drunk in the morning,* she remembered. *Okay.*

"What happened?" Marian asked, stretching and yawning.

"You passed out," said Carol without turning. "Don't you remember anything?"

"I remember we talked about Lewis. Then it's a blank."

"Oh. Well, you passed out and I rolled you onto the couch and let you sleep. That's all."

Very good, thought Marian. Except that I remember and she remembers, and both of us knows that the other remembers. But we will never talk about it, and this pretense will make it unnecessary for us to make excuses to each other. And I couldn't explain it anyway ...

"I'm going to take a shower," she said, and walked into the bathroom. She dropped her robe and stepped into the shower booth, pulling the curtain behind her. She adjusted the spray to a chilly temperature and gasped as she stepped under it. Gradually, the cold water drove the fuzzy cobwebs from her brain.

I'm not a Lesbian, she thought. I suppose that's a good thing to know. Worry about it all my life if I didn't find out. Funny though ... not a bad sensation, soft tingly little pleasure, nice enough for a change. But kind of like ... like eating ice cream when you're starved for a big juicy steak. You quiet your appetite, but a woman has a deeper hunger that another woman just can't satisfy. Funny about Carol, no hesitation at all, no awkwardness either. Was she telling the truth? Never before?

Marian turned off the shower and began soaping herself. She generated a thick hoard of lather low on her stomach and spread it upward. She enjoyed the slick feel of her hands on her flesh as she spread the lather on her arms, breasts, and legs. Sensuous, she thought, a woman's hands feel softer. Sure, a woman was made for love; a man had other things to do with himself.

She turned on the shower, stepped under it, and started rinsing her body. She started humming. She felt good, even about Dee. He would come back—

Zzzzzp! Marian felt a coldness on her back as the shower curtain was jerked aside. Carol, she thought, what now? Fun and games so early in the morning? She sighed and turned off the shower. "Close the curtain, Carol."

Someone chuckled. It was a male voice, and it wasn't Dee's. She knew whose voice it was, and the knowledge sent shivers of ice all the way up her spine. She tried to scream, but her voice was a low moan deep in her throat.

"Turn around," said Lewis. "I've seen this side."

Slowly she turned. He stood there with his cold unblinking eyes on her. His mouth sober and mirthless. His shirt was covered with bits of leaves and grass; his pants were wrinkled and dirty. In his hand was the gun Dee had given her. It pointed at a spot two inches below her navel.

"What ..." her lips were dry and she licked them. "What do you want?"

"You."

His voice was flat, like a rock thunked into a dead tree.

"Pack a bag," he said. "Just a few clothes. Leave a note for your husband. I'll tell you what to write."

Insane, she thought. Mad. She made a move to cover her sex, then decided it was pointless. It wasn't his eyes that would kill her, anyway.

"Where—?" she began.

"A place I know. Private." He almost smiled, then his mouth straightened. "Hurry. Before everybody wakes up."

Carol? Marian wondered but said nothing. She must have gone to her house for something. All the better. Rescue ...

Lewis jabbed with the gun. "Move. Pack."

Humor him, she told herself. I can leave some hint in the note to Dee. And Carol will know the note's a phony. She walked stiffly ahead of Lewis, her back itchy with the knowledge of the gun. She opened the door of the bathroom and stepped out—

Carol lay near the kitchen door like a collapsed ragdoll. A stream of blood ran from her hair and across the sloping floor. It was a long stream, and growing longer. Marian opened her mouth and started to scream. An explosion in the back of her head sent her falling forward into a black pit.

10

Joe Forrest knew he was in a strange bed. It was a soft puffy bed, the kind that surrounds you when you lie in it. Joe preferred his own hard mattress.

He lay without moving, trying to remember what had happened during the last hours of the party. He had started drinking straight shots after that excruciating scene with Dee Morgan, and from that point on the light in Joe's mind had steadily dimmed. He vaguely remembered standing by while Gloria, the politician's mistress, jumped unclad into the lake. That husband of Betty's had floundered in after her, fully dressed, and of course the dolt had had to be dragged out...

But that did not solve the question of where he was. In a woman's bedroom; he could tell that by the smell of perfume, cosmetics, by the thousand other subtle aromas which the female of the species uses to snare the male. But which female?

He opened his eyes. Raw daylight stabbed his brain and he squeezed them shut again. Headache, too. He wished he were in his own bedroom, able to stretch out his hand and start the coffee, or find the hangover remedy without opening his eyes ...

Suddenly he became aware of warmth beside him. So she was in bed with him. Now, if she were someone he knew—and the complex of familiar odors hinted that she was—then he could learn her identity with his eyes closed. Slowly he stretched out his hand and touched flesh. What part? Oh, a knee. She was facing him with her knees drawn up against her chest. He moved his hand down and felt the prickle of a bristly calf. Let's see now, who do I know who sleeps in a foetal position? And has hairy legs?

He needed more clues. He slid his hand upward; he couldn't get any information out of her feet, who the hell looks at a woman's feet? Some characters went ape over feet, but Joe was strictly a normal man. His searching hand closed over a resilient mound. Ah. Not the politician's mistress ... not Carol... not Marian ...

The thought of Marian brought a stab of regret. He had been hoping that it might be Marian, knowing too that the hope was futile. She had told him that again last night: "Joe, it was nice, but I've had it with playing around. I hope we can be friends, but—"

He was squeezing the flesh absently while he thought, like a boxer kneading a sponge-rubber ball. And now there were signs of life, a slight thrust of the nipple against his palm.

Now that he had started the game, Joe wanted to finish it. But the breast told him nothing. He moved his hand up, touched the throat, the lips, he felt the teeth—

"Ouch!" He jerked his hand away and opened his eyes. The woman was looking at him, her dark eyes crinkled with amusement. "Betty! What's the idea?"

She smiled. "The idea was to get you back where you were. You were doing fine."

She took his hand and laid it back on her breast. Joe let it lie and studied Betty's face. She looked bright enough; she must have stayed fairly sober. But damned if he could remember—

"How'd I happen to get here?"

She raised her brows. "You don't remember helping me bring Carl home? When we got here we decided you were too drunk to drive home."

Carl. The husband. And here he was in the man's

house, in bed with his wife. He sat up. "Where is he?"

"Relax. The door's locked. He's on the living-room couch."

Joe held his breath and heard muffled snoring through the closed door. From the sound of it, Carl was beyond the reach of any disturbance. Anyway, as he remembered from his last affair with Betty, the man was indifferent to whom his wife took to bed. Still you never could be sure ...

"Come on, Joe," she said. "Cozy up."

He lay back, and Betty scooted over and put her head on his pillow. He could see the pores in her nose, and the hint of yellow in the whites of her eyes. Her breath had a sour morning odor, but he realized that his own breath probably smelled worse.

He turned away and lit a cigarette. He lay smoking, looking at the ceiling, conscious of this nude woman stretched out beside him. It failed to fill him with anticipatory joy. He and Betty had had their fling; to repeat it would be like seeing a re-run of an old movie.

"What else happened last night?"

"The usual," she said with a throaty chuckle.

Joe turned to her in surprise. "Really?"

"Really." She arched her body against him like a fed cat stretching itself before a warm fire. "You were babbling drunk, Joe. But your instincts carried you through."

Good old rutting instinct, he thought; about time it did something for me.

"What did I babble about?"

"You called me Marian a few times."

He stiffened. "Marian?"

She lay her hand on his stomach and began moving it in slow circles. "Yep. Marian. I let it pass since it seemed to help you. The result was the same."

"Well, well," he mused. "Marian Smith, an old

girlhood sweetheart. Funny I should mention her name."

"Yeah, funny. Don't try to kid me."

"I'm not. Who the hell else—?"

"Marian Morgan, that's who else. You asked me if I thought you'd make a good husband; I was about to get up and try on my old wedding gown when I learned you were talking about Marian Morgan."

He turned, "Oh, now, listen—"

"It's true. You said you'd goofed off long enough. Time you stopped running an obstacle course from one woman's bed to another before you got perforated by an angry husband. My God, I thought, is this the same Joe who gave me that line about not buying a cow when milk is free—?"

"You know how it is when you're drunk," he said.

"I know. *In vino veritas.*"

"Don't believe it. I lie like hell when I'm drunk."

"Well, you'd better not get drunk around Dee Morgan.

I doubt if he'd believe you."

"I know." Joe sighed heavily. He had never before let a woman drive him to maudlin fantasy. It sounded as though he had been in pretty bad condition last night. "A man in my position has no business drinking."

"You really shouldn't," said Betty. "I like you better sober. Nice, strong and ... hard."

She pinched his stomach, then threw her thigh over his and pulled him into the embrace of her legs. She gripped him tightly and began moving in unmistakable invitation while her hands worked hard, hard. He tried to push down the rising urge of passion ...

"Betty, your husband's right out there."

"He won't wake up."

Joe listened to uninterrupted snores. "You can't be sure."

"It doesn't matter if he does. But if you want to I'll go hold a pillow over his head."

"Oh, hell." Almost reluctantly, he rolled over and pulled her to him. His hand just touched her back and she threw herself against him, clinging like flypaper. She seemed to have sprouted on extra set of arms and legs; she was touching him all over, kissing his face with early-morning taste on her lips, moaning endearments, and finally giving tongue to urgent moans.

He wanted to tell her for Heaven's sake to quiet down, because she'd wake people three houses away, not to mention her husband. Even if Carl wasn't dangerous, Joe dreaded getting mixed up in a sticky deal like that.

But he soon forgot Carl, for Betty was a woman crazed. She tossed herself about with wild abandon. Together they wallowed in the great, soft downy mattress until he thought he must be about to drive her through it, onto the floor ...

Joe froze as a knock sounded on the door. "Betty?"

It was Carl's voice, low and hesitant. "Betty?" he repeated.

"Oh, damn!" whispered Betty. She was breathing hard, and a fine film of sweat bedewed her face. She never stopped moving, and her words came out in hoarse gasps.

"What ... the ... hell do ... you ... want?"

The voice became plaintive. "I can't find the bromo."

She stopped moving. "It's in the medicine cabinet, where the hell did you think?"

"Oh." Joe heard a shuffle of footsteps as Carl walked away. He felt Betty's hand rubbing his back, felt the movement begin again. Suddenly he realized that his desire, never very strong, was now totally absent. "It's gone, Betty."

"I can bring it back."

"No," he said. "I can't make this scene."

"Yes! You can't leave me now!"

He tried to get up, but her arms gripped his neck, her heels dug into his back. He grunted and tried to unclasp her hands from behind his neck, but she clung like a drowning woman. He tried to break the grip of her legs, but she crossed her ankles and squeezed until he was gasping for breath. Hers was a desperate strength, and the sounds which issued from her throat were those of a madwoman, hoarse and incoherent.

Finally, Joe stopped struggling and let his body go limp. "Hadn't you heard, Betty? A man can't be raped."

For a full minute she did not answer. She kept moving, biting her lower lip with the effort. Her hair lay damp on her forehead, her body grew slack with perspiration. Finally she seemed to realize she'd lost him; she relaxed with a long ragged sigh and watched him rise from the bed.

"You're getting old, Joe," she said with derision. "Better check in at the county home."

Silently, Joe found his scattered clothing and started dressing. As he buttoned his shirt, he said without rancor: "Maybe you're right, Betty. I could send my assistant out. He's only sixteen."

"Send him," she said. "I'll wait right here."

He looked at her. Her body sank deeply into the mattress, her breasts flattened out on her chest and her knees were drawn up and wide apart. On her mouth was a crooked smile, and in her eyes a look of scorn.

Scorn didn't bother him, but he was suddenly eager to leave her.

He picked up his jacket, slipped on his shoes without tying them, stuck his necktie in his pocket, and walked to the door.

"Goodbye, Betty," he said as he opened it.

"Don't forget to send your boy."

He closed the door without answering. Carl was sitting in the kitchen drinking coffee, his sparse fringe of hair standing straight up around his head. Joe felt a stab of dread as the man looked up and spoke in a tone of forced heartiness:

"Joe. Have a cup of coffee."

Joe kept walking. "Going home, Carl."

"Wait."

Joe paused as Carl pushed himself up and walked toward him, belting his bathrobe. He dreaded the coming scene. It wouldn't be violence, because Carl wasn't the type to kill a cockroach, but Joe was sure it would be distasteful.

"I wanted to say I appreciate your helping me home last night," said Carl.

"Was nothing," said Joe brusquely, and turned to go.

Carl caught his arm, and Joe thought: My God, how soft and warm those fingers are. "I wanted to say, you're welcome to come back anytime."

Curiosity momentarily overcame Joe's distaste. He frowned at Carl. "You know where I slept last night?"

"Well... I was three sheets in the wind as they say. I..." He started to smile, then licked his lips. "I know, sure ... can't blame anybody, everybody drunk, perfectly innocent—"

"You know damn well it wasn't innocent, don't you?"

Carl reddened. "Well, I—"

"You knew what was going on in there when you knocked, didn't you? Didn't you?" Suddenly angry, Joe seized the front of Carl's robe and bunched it in his hand. He felt as though he'd been used; he felt like a male prostitute.

"Goddamn! What the hell kind of husband are you? Why the hell don't you get mad?" He shook the little man until his head bobbed up and down. "Why don't you fight?"

Carl's eyes bulged with terror. He bawled, "Betty! Betty!"

She ran into the room naked, her eyes flashing fire. "What are you doing, Joe Forrest? Why pick on him?" She walked up to Joe, her eyes flashing fire, "Why get mad at him because you can't make it in bed?"

"Oh, for Christ's sake!"

Joe spun on his heel and strode out. He felt dirty. As he closed the door, he saw that Betty had thrown her arm across her husband's shoulder and was smoothing his sparse hair.

Jesus, he thought, as he got into his car. What a mess. Worst morning I've had in years.

As he drove home, he thought: I didn't even enjoy it. No kick, and a lot of misery. Maybe it's time to quit, get out of the rat race, stop messing with women who have to fit you in between taking the kids to school and fixing the husband's supper. Get a good woman, settle down. Best woman I know is Marian, and she's having none of it. But still, never say die ...

He thought of Marian all the way home. He felt an aching desire to see her, simply to talk to her. When he entered his house, he saw that it was only seven. Too early, he thought. Nobody would be up.

Well, it wouldn't hurt to call. They had left the party early; maybe Dee had to be in court today. And judging from the way he had dragged her across the lawn last night, there might have been a fight after they had got home. Marian might be just in the mood to listen to what Joe had to say.

His heart thumping, he picked up the phone and dialed. The phone started ringing, and to calm himself he reached for a cigarette and lit it. Maybe they're asleep, he thought. But no, who the hell could sleep through ten rings? Maybe they're occupied—

The thought brought a stab of jealousy. He waited three more rings, then he hung up and sat smoking, staring into space. I can't just sit here, he thought. Can't relax. Maybe a swim ...

The swim was invigorating, but it only increased his restlessness. Still wearing his trunks he boarded one of the new cabin cruisers. The wiring had been repaired so the cruiser would run, but the upholstery was still slashed and torn.

Damn crazy kid, thought Joe, as he steered for the main channel. By God, if he ever comes back to this part of the country ...

He stood up behind the wheel and peered over the top of the cabin, letting the wind blow in his face. The sun was just rising over the hills in the south and the lake was like a sheet of glass. The cruiser skimmed along as though through air, leaving the sound of the engine behind. Joe saw the two buttes that jutted like gateposts at the entrance of Glade Cove. Without hesitation, he twisted the wheel and banked toward it, laughing into the wind. He felt like a kid on his first day of summer vacation.

Who were you trying to kid, Forrest? You knew you were going to try to see Marian.

The cove looked dead and sleepy. That was natural, thought Joe. In each of those houses, there must be at least two throbbing hangovers from last night's party. He rounded the point of land and looked at Marian's redwood cabin, feeling like a boy who rides his new bike past his girl's house.

Well, Dee's car was gone. What luck, what joy! *I'll go up and ask her out for a cruise, and then if she comes, I'll ask that big, important question I've been saving for thirty-five years...*

He came in slowly to Dee's floating dock. He reversed

the engine, brought the hull to rest against the pier opposite Dee's small inboard. He jumped out, tied up the boat, and walked silently up the stairs.

Risky, he thought, Dee might have merely lent his car to someone. But the hell with it. Joe's heart was pounding as he walked to the porch. The screen door was unlocked. He pulled it open and saw that the kitchen door was ajar.

"Marian, you home?" he called softly through the gap.

He heard a faint movement inside. He pushed on the kitchen door. "Marian, it's—"

He choked off when he saw Carol on the floor. Then a movement caught his eye and he looked up into the iceblue eyes of Lewis. An explosion seemed to fill the room. A tremendous blow struck Joe high in the chest. It knocked him back through the door, sent him staggering across the porch. He tried to grab the railing but the landscape tilted and he went over. The ground seemed to float slowly up to catch his body ...

When Joe woke up, he was surprised to see the sun still slanting low through the trees. Leaves and bits of grass stuck to the blood which covered the upper part of his body. He was beneath the steps which led down to the dock.

He looked at himself and saw the oozing hole in his shoulder. Oozing, he thought. That was supposed to mean that an artery wasn't hit. He moved his shoulder and nearly fainted from the sudden grating pain. *Oh, Jesus, bullet smashed the collar bone, can't even move ...*

He lay back and tried to push the cobwebs from his mind. Lewis had shot him. Lewis was in Marian's house. Dee was gone. So—the kid was after Marian.

Oh, Jesus, how much time have I wasted ... ?

Joe pulled himself from beneath the steps and pulled himself to a kneeling position. He looked toward the house, then saw a movement at the top of the ridge. Marian walked in front, dressed in a bright print skirt and a white blouse. Lewis walked two paces behind, and had his right hand wrapped in a towel. The bastard had a gun on her...

Joe caught the railing and with his good hand pulled himself to his feet. He knew he was too weak to make it to the top of the ridge. He doubted if he could even make it to the house, because that was uphill too. *Well, the bastard must have a boat stashed over there on the other cove. If I can make it to mine, I can outrun him ...*

Slowly, Joe made his way down to the cruiser. The movement seemed to speed up the bleeding, but Joe did not worry about it.

He was several minutes starting his engine, because it took both hands. Each time he used his right arm, the grating pain washed over him. Then he had to stop and fight off a fainting spell. That killed five or ten minutes. He eased away from the dock and headed out of the cove. The landscape tilted and blurred before his eyes, but he managed to reach open water. It stretched like a mirror to the green wilderness of the opposite shore two miles away. All empty, featureless...

No. There was a small outboard a mile from that other shore. He could make out the faint wake leading back from the boat. That must be Lewis, had to be ...

Joe opened the throttle and pointed the cruiser at the speck. Roaring into the wind, he looked down and saw the blood pouring freely from his chest, soaking his trunks, and running down his legs. God, ought to stop up that damn hole, damned eyes going bad, like a light when the current falters.

He glanced behind him and saw that his wake had made a snakelike pattern across the lake. Grating his teeth, he set the chains which would hold the cruiser on a straight course. Halfway across, he saw that the little boat had been beached in an almost hidden niche, too small to be called a cove. He saw the tiny figures of Marian and Lewis just as they disappeared into the trees ...

Suddenly the world tilted and faded out. His head fell forward and struck the wheel. He fought to open his eyes, tried to push himself up. Come on, Joe, come on. Get up there, get up. Up!

It was a long time before he found the strength. He raised his head in time to see the jumbled mass of rocks and trees rushing toward him. Too fast! He made a grab for the throttle, but not in time. The bank was ten yards off—

He squeezed his eyes shut and gripped the wheel, thinking, at least I'll mark the spot where they went in.

He heard a shrieking crash, felt a jolting pain in his head. A loud roaring filled his ears, then came silence—

11

Dee sat in the camp director's office and counted the number of times the telephone rang in his home. He reached twelve, then heard the operator's voice.

"There's no answer, sir. Shall I keep trying?"

"Yes. Keep trying."

Dee hung up the phone and looked at his watch. Eight o'clock. The woman should be up. Or Carol should be, at least. But neither answered. Not for the first time that day, since that morning, Dee felt the cold chill of fear.

"No answer?"

Dee looked at the camp director. Bill Fisher wore

horn-rimmed glasses on his round face and had a habit of talking to adults as he talked to children. He would be a nice young man, Dee thought, if he didn't worry so much about his fingernails. Bill was filing them now with a shiny silver file which he clipped to the pocket of his khaki shirt when he wasn't using it.

"No," said Dee. "No answer."

For a moment he sat there, lacing his fingers and squeezing them so tightly his knuckles popped. The Dexamyl gave him energy, but he had nothing to do except wait and try to reach Marian, or someone. Dee did not look at the camp director, and Bill Fisher did not look at Dee. A wall of embarrassment had risen between them, because Fisher had been there when Sharon tearfully had blurted out her story:

".... Up there with a naked man, Daddy! And she wasn't dressed either—!"

Dee had never known such rage. Rage at Marian, and rage at the man. At first he had assumed it was Joe Forrest, then he and Fisher had talked to the boy who had brought the story. That's when Dee's fear had begun. Because the boy had described Lewis. Dee's fear had grown when the boy said he had visited the ridge again the following week, and had seen the same man watching the house through binoculars.

Lewis is psychotic, thought Dee now, remembering those strange fixed eyes. No telling what he might do. Capable of anything. Suddenly Dee remembered something else. *My gun, that broken picture. Oh, Lord...*

"The sheriff!" said Dee abruptly.

Fisher jumped. "Sir?"

"I'm going to call the sheriff."

"Oh. The sheriff." Fisher watched Dee from the corner of his eyes as he dialed the long distance operator and gave her the sheriff's number.

"I'll pay for these calls," said Dee. "Send me a bill."

"Oh..." Fisher made a deprecating gesture with his nail file, but Dee knew the bill would be sent, carefully itemized, with margins even and no erasures. He knew Fisher's type.

There was a click on the other end of the line, then a breathless female voice said hello. Like most year-round lake-dwellers, the sheriff operated a summer business in order to survive during the long moneyless winter. His happened to be a short-order cafe, and Dee recognized the voice of his harried waitress.

"Is Sheriff Powell there?" he asked.

"No. Call back at ten."

"Wait!" He said quickly since the woman had seemed about to hang up. "This is important. Where is he?"

"There was some houses broken into last night and he's looking into it."

"Well... Is the deputy there?"

"He's looking, too."

Dee clenched his fists. Damn, everybody out looking for a lousy burglar and Marian might be in danger. "Look, can you get in touch with him? My wife doesn't answer the phone and it's possible something's happened to her. I'm DeWitt Morgan. We've got a cabin out on Glade Cove."

"Got any neighbors? Can't you have them check?"

Dee forced himself to keep patient. "I called our next door neighbor, Carol... Mrs. Carter doesn't answer either."

"Uh-huh." The woman didn't sound impressed. "Glade Cove is where they had that big party last night, women swimming naked, drunk till dawn. Maybe they just can't get outa bed."

Dee set his teeth and spoke in carefully measured tones. "I was at the party. My wife came home early. So did my neighbor. Will you please get in touch with the sheriff and have him stop at my cabin."

"Okay. I'll tell him when he gets back."

"Now, for God's sake! Something may have happened—!"

"What makes you think so?"

Dee was swelled up to shout, but her question caught him without an answer. He let his wind expire slowly through his lips. What the hell could he say? That she'd been seen naked on the ridge with a suspected maniac, and that said maniac had been eyeing the house for a week. No, he couldn't say that...

"We have seen a prowler in our neighborhood a couple of times—"

"Did you report it?"

"Let me finish! Then, night before last our house was broken into and a gun was stolen."

"Did you report it?"

"Goddamn it! Are you the sheriff?"

"Now if you're going to swear, Mr. Morgan—"

"No, we didn't report it. I didn't know... look. Will you call the sheriff? My wife's in danger!"

"Hold on."

She was gone one minute, then: "He doesn't answer his radio."

"You didn't give him time."

"Well, I figure he mighta stopped off to check his trotline, and that takes an hour. And I got all these customers here who—"

Slam! Dee cradled the receiver with a jolt that brought Fisher upright in his chair. He opened his mouth as though to complain. Dee glared, and the man lowered his eyes and concentrated again on his manicure.

Dee searched his mind frantically, trying to think of someone ... Of course! Joe Forrest. The fact he had slept with Marian did not seem important now. The man was interested in her; he would be willing to help if she were in danger. That was all that mattered.

His gas pump attendant answered the phone. "Naw, he ain't here. One of the cruisers is missing so I figure he's gone out for a little spin."

Oh, Lord, thought Dee.

"Look, this is Dee Morgan. Tell him to go out to my cabin when he gets back."

"Will do."

"Tell him Marian needs—"

But the boy had hung up. Oh, hell, thought Dee. He lowered the receiver, gently this time. A heavy weight of fatigue lay on his shoulders; yet the drug made it impossible to sit still. He knew his calls had accomplished nothing. The woman might or might not tell the sheriff, and when he returned. Joe Forrest might or might not go out to the cabin, even if he returned in the next few minutes. Maybe Dee had done too good a job of scaring him.

He jumped up. "Only one thing to do. Go back."

Bill Fisher nodded sagely. "Go back."

"I'll have to leave Sharon here. Will she be—?"

"She'll be perfectly safe," said the director in a stiff, formal tone, somewhat injured.

"Yes. Well, if any of those calls come through, you know what to say."

"I'll deliver the message." He rose and held out his perfectly manicured hand. "I certainly hope nothing's wrong, Mr. Morgan. I hope you find everything all right."

"Thanks," said Dee, pumping the hand. "And send me a bill for those calls."

Then he found Sharon, kissed her goodbye, and jumped into his car. A hundred-twenty miles through hill country to the lake. That was a two-hour drive if he pushed hell out of it. And he would.

An hour and forty-five minutes later he pulled to a stop in front of his cabin. He left the car without bothering to close the door and trotted quickly up the steps. Then he saw something that made his heart stop.

Brown droplets stained the porch floor. They made a trail leading to the steps. Blood.

For a moment Dee thought he was going to faint; he staggered and nearly fell, then he caught himself on the railing. A moment later an icy calm crept over him. His worst fears had been realized. Now he had nothing to do but act.

He pulled open the screen door and pushed on the kitchen door. He grunted with shock when he saw the figure on the floor.

"Marian!" he cried. Then he saw that it wasn't Marian at all. It was Carol wearing Marian's housecoat. He gave a sigh of relief, and felt ashamed of his relief. The girl was hurt, breathing noisily, dried blood caking her scalp.

He searched the house and found it empty. No other sign of violence. He returned to Carol, then ran to the sink and soaked a dishcloth with cold water. He bent and washed the blood from her head. Parting the hair, he saw a raised welt about a half-inch broad. There was a two-inch gap in her scalp, but the bleeding had stopped. A dozen or so stitches would fix her. Now he had to wake her up and find out what had happened to Marian.

He wet a clean cloth and lifted her head into his lap. Gently he wiped her face, then parted the robe and ran the wet cloth over her breasts and stomach. Her eyelids fluttered, and she moaned softly.

"Carol," he said. "Wake up. This is Dee."

"Dee ... darling." She fumbled for his hand, found it, and pressed it against her breasts. "Don't go away—"

"Where's Marian?"

Her eyes flew open. "Marian?" She looked bewildered. She raised her head, then groaned and lay slowly back in his lap. "Oh ... my head ... what the hell happened?"

"I found you on the floor. Marian's gone. Can you remember anything?"

"I... Yes. I remember I was making coffee. I heard a tap on the window. I raised up to look out and felt a jolt on my head. Next thing, here you are."

Dee realized the girl was hurt, and tried to keep his patience. "Carol, Marian's missing and there's blood on the porch. You know anything about that?"

"Oh, God. Lewis!"

"Did you see him?"

"No, but... Marian told me about him. Night before last he chased her into my house. Wouldn't leave. She called Joe and he came and got her."

Dee groaned. "So that's why—"

"Yes. That's why she stayed with him."

Dee stood up. "Carol, there's codeine in the medicine cabinet. Take a pill and then get to a doctor. I'm going to see where that blood trail leads to."

"You want me to call the sheriff?"

"Hell, no. That's a waste of time."

On the porch he leaned out and saw the same brown stains on the grass below. He ran down the steps and found that the trail led to the dock and ended there. Somebody had taken a boat from here; it could have been Lewis. Must have been ...

Quickly, he cast off the ropes on his launch. He got behind the wheel and heard Carol shout, "Wait! I'll go with you!" She ran down the steps, her breasts bouncing beneath the loose fit of one of Marian's dresses. Dee assumed she hadn't had time to put on anything under it. He waited until she was seated beside him, then he gunned his engine and roared out of the cove. He spoke his thoughts aloud as he steered toward the main channel.

"There's twenty-thousand acres of wilderness on the other side of the lake—owned by the power company. Not a road in it, not a house, nothing. If I were kidnaping a woman and wanted to be alone with her, that's where I'd take her."

Carol gasped. "Kidnaping—!"

Dee frowned at her. "You think she went willingly?"

"Well, I—"

"He wouldn't have bothered to slug you, dammit! Not if she had made a date with him." Dee reached the channel and steered for the opposite shore, trying to shut out the vision of Marian tramping through the woods with an armed maniac. He did not know how much time he had. He wished he were sure that Marian realized how deadly a man like Lewis could be.

Two hundred yards from the opposite shore, he banked his boat and steered parallel to the wild, rocky shoreline. To Carol, he said: "Help me watch the bank. He's probably hidden his boat, but he may not have wiped out his keel mark. Let's hope not."

And let's hope he's not too far away, he thought. With all these little coves and inlets, there must be close to a hundred miles of shoreline on this side. It would take days to search it thoroughly. Then there was all that jumbled wilderness...

Fifteen minutes later Carol shouted: "There!"

Dee saw the deep gouge in the bank at almost the same moment. No outboard made that, he thought, then he saw the wrecked cruiser almost hidden under the trees. God! Some damn fool must have come in at top speed. Climbed fifty feet up the bank and wedged his bow between two trees. Another tree had snapped off and fallen across the cabin, its branches trailing over the deck.

Suddenly he recognized the boat. One of Joe Forrest's cruisers. *Well, I'll be damned. Could it be ....?*

Dee swung into shore, grounded the launch, and jumped out. He ran to the cruiser and climbed the ladder. Joe lay on the slanted deck, curled beneath the seat as though he had been trying to pull himself up when his strength had failed. Dee saw a huge lump on his forehead where his head must have struck the wheel. Then he saw the ragged, crusted hole in his shoulder. Dee bent down and felt the feeble pulse. He called to Carol: "Bring water. He's still alive."

A minute later, Carol threw her long bare legs over the side and climbed aboard. She carried the thermos jug from Dee's launch. She gasped when she saw Joe.

"He's been shot," said Dee.

She nodded and kneeled beside him. Without hesitation, she grasped the hem of her dress, ripped it nearly to her waist, tore it across, then ripped it down to the hem again. Dee noted absently that his hunch had been right; she hadn't worn anything under the dress. He fidgeted as he watched her wet the cloth and clean the skin around the wound. At first, he was comforted by the thought that since Joe had caught the bullet, it had been his blood on the steps. So Marian wasn't hurt—yet. The last word filled him with dread. If Lewis had shot Joe, probably with intent to kill, the fiend would not hesitate to kill Marian if she tried to escape. Or even if she didn't. The man was paranoic; he could imagine she was planning something and that would be the end.

"Hurry," he said to Carol. "Throw water on his face. See if you can wake him."

Carol shot him an annoyed glance over her shoulder, then soaked the rag and wrung it out in Joe's face.

Joe moved and groaned.

"Joe. This is Morgan."

"Morgan?" Joe grunted. "The bastard got her!"

"I know. Which way'd they go?"

Joe opened his eyes and squinted in an effort to focus on Dee. "You found the spot... by the wreck?"

"Yes. That's how we found it."

Joe smiled as though that pleased him. Then he looked at Carol for the first time. He smiled at her too. "Carol, you're looking better than usual. Like a lovely angel."

"Just lie still, Joe." She spoke in a crisp tone, but she flushed with pleasure and very gently began bathing his forehead.

Dee felt his skin crawl with impatience. He knew Joe was still groggy from the crash, but he couldn't stand around much longer. Each passing moment increased Marian's peril.

"Joe," he said, "can't you tell me which way they went?"

Joe frowned, tried to lift his arm and point, then gasped with pain and lowered it. He nodded his head toward the right of the boat. "They disappeared on that side."

"All right. Can you tell me anything else."

"He's got a gun."

"I know that."

"He doesn't hesitate to use it."

"I know that, too."

"Well... I hope ... you find her." His eyes closed and he breathed raggedly.

"Stay with him, Carol," said Dee. He started over the side of the boat, then paused. Because he wasn't sure what would happen in the woods, he said, "Joe's a good man."

"I know." She looked at him and seemed to

understand. "I'll tell him you said that—when he wakes up."

Dee ran to his launch and seized his three-foot-long fishing gaff. The barbed hook gleamed in the sun. Dee gripped it tightly in his big hand, and plunged into the woods. He found a trail of scuffed leaves, and started following it up the slope.

If he's hurt her, thought Dee, swinging the gaff, I'll sink this thing into his neck and rip out his throat.

For the tenth time in an hour, Lewis parted his concealing screen of brush and peered into the ravine that hid the cave. He was ready to scream from frustration.

Of all the rotten luck, thought Lewis. Who'd have thought those damn-fool college kids would pick this particular ravine for a goddamn all-day beerbust? They had the damn beer keg set up not five yards from the entrance of his cave. He watched one of the boys draw off a pint of the foamy liquid and drain it. At ten o'clock in the morning, for God's sake! What a hell of a time to start a party!

Lewis fingered the gun and felt a fiery urge to put a bullet into the belly of the drinker, a sweatshirted, burr-haircut blond with sandals. But Lewis knew that if he shot one, he would have to shoot all of them—the other boys and the three girls—and he did not have that many bullets. Patience, he told himself. She's yours now. Lewis lowered the gun and looked at Marian, hidden beneath the overhanging brush beside him.

A strip of tape bound her mouth so she could not scream. Her hands were tied behind her with his ski-rope. The same rope bound her feet. On her knees with her head bowed, she made Lewis think of something in a movie he had seen: Joan of Arc, bound to the stake, receiving a blessing from the priest.

"Are the ropes too tight?" he asked in a whisper.

The only sign she had heard him was a slight flaring of her nostrils.

"I'm sorry about the delay," he said. "I had your home all ready but these punks loused it up."

She turned away from him, wrinkling her nose as though from a foul odor. Lewis felt a surge of anger. He'd show her soon. Damn soon.

He looked back at the college students. They represented the last of a series of setbacks which had begun early that morning. First the party had held him off. Next, Carol had been with Marian. Then while he had lain there waiting for a chance to go down, he had gotten drowsy. He had slept, and had not awakened until daylight. He had hoped to make off with her in the dark, but he couldn't wait another day. Then everything had gone fine for a while; he had cooled Carol before she could scream. He had surprised Marian in the shower with that lovely body glowing like a rose. But she had screamed at the sight of Carol, and Lewis had struck her in panic. It had taken him an hour to wake her up and before she had had a chance to more than dress, that damned boat peddler had showed up.

Lewis smiled as he remembered the solid kick of the gun butt in his hand, the astounded look on Joe's face as he went back through the door like a man kicked by a horse. He'd never fool around with Marian again...

Yet the gunshot had made things worse, really. Lewis had to leave at once... No time for Marian to write the note which would throw off pursuit, no time for her to pack, no time to bring Carol along to serve him and Marian and keep her from talking. He had wanted to go down and put a bullet in the head of Joe Forrest, just to be sure, but a second gunshot would surely have attracted attention.

And now those goddam students...

He heard the blond boy say something about wood, then saw him take one of the girls by the hand. She was a brunette with short hair, clinging white toreador pants and a white jersey so tight you could see the brassiere strap cutting into her back.

Oh, oh. Coming this way, coming right up this hill.

He lifted the gun and flicked off the safety; he would put a bullet right in the gut of that college kid if he tried to get his wood here. Just a few more steps, just a little bit closer...

Twenty feet away, the boy suddenly flopped on the grass and jerked the girl down with him. Lewis could hear their laughter, but the tall grass hid them. He rose to his knees and saw the boy flat on his back, the girl lying across him, her lips glued to his. The boy's hand ran up and fumbled beneath the jersey. The girl made no move to stop him as the bra came loose.

Old lovers, thought Lewis. That was apparent from the speed of the operation. Must be something in the air to give them the urge to merge so early in the morning.

Watching them, Lewis felt a growing excitement. The girl had puffed up the jersey, and was wallowing on the boy with her bare breasts against his chest; they kissed and rolled their heads from side to side; the boy got busy with his hands again, unzipping the toreadors, pushing them down off her hips.

Lewis was breathing hard. He inched silently up beside Marian and pointed with his gun barrel.

"You see them?" he whispered in her ear.

She shook her head without looking up.

"Well, look at them, dammit." He seized her hair and jerked back her head. Her blouse was damp with perspiration. He saw it run down her neck and disappear between her breasts. Her flesh was warm against him, making the blood throb in his veins.

"You see them?" he whispered again.

This time she nodded once. He let go of her hair and she slumped back into her original position.

He looked back at the students; they had reversed their positions. The sight was more than Lewis could bear. He had with him a woman for whom he had risked everything, even his life. Damned if he would sit and watch another man enjoy himself while he waited.

But he would have to move further inland. He had heard the faint throb of a passing inboard not ten minutes before. Though he had hidden his boat well, he could not take the risk of untying Marian this close to the lake.

He loosed Marian's feet and whispered: "We're going to move on. Walk ahead of me around the ridge— quietly. I'll be pointing this gun right at your back."

She started forward, bending at the waist to avoid a low crab apple branch. She staggered suddenly and a twig popped. She turned and looked back at him, her eyes wide with fear, then pointed to her ankles. They were red and swollen where the ski-rope had bound them.

"I'll fix that," he said. He kneeled behind her and rubbed her ankles with his free hand. He rested his forehead against her buttock and felt its faint, muscular trembling beneath her skirt. He slid his hand up her calf, over the knee, and up her inner thigh. Her legs were damp and hot. His hand reached the limit of its journey and paused a moment; her muscles went rigid as steel and she trembled like a young mare being saddled for the first time.

He rose and said hoarsely, "Move."

They walked for about a half-mile, over the ridge,

across a small ravine, up the next ridge. He guided her silently through the best cover as a mahout guides his elephant, turning her right or left by a touch of his gun barrel on her shoulder. Her blouse clung to her sweating back.

They were going down the next ridge when they came to a place where a few decades ago the earth had begun to slide into the ravine, then had stopped. It had left a half circle of flat grassy earth in the hillside. On three sides the bank rose steeply, the fourth side was bordered by an impenetrable hazelbush thicket. He tapped her shoulder and pointed down.

She went down the steep bank, slipping and sliding, unable to balance herself with her hands tied behind her back. Near the bottom, she fell and rolled, her brown legs flopping as she turned over and over. She rolled onto the grass and lay still. Her dress was twisted around her hips, showing white panties against brown legs.

Lewis tasted panic in his mouth as he leaped down the bank. He did not want this prize damaged before he had had a chance to enjoy it.

She was conscious, but her eyes were squeezed shut and there were tear-tracks in the dust on her cheekbones. He untied her hands, gently removed the gag from her mouth, and backed away.

"I'm sorry you fell," he said. "I should have untied your hands."

She shot him a look of surprise but said nothing. She was swallowing often, running her tongue over her lips.

"You can talk now. We're safe." He smiled. "You can even scream if you want. There's nobody around."

She ignored him and began massaging her wrists.

"Marian," he said, trying to make his voice gentle,

"you might as well be nice to me. You aren't going to get away."

She turned her head slowly and looked at him. For Lewis, it was like looking deep into a fiery pit of hatred, hissing, bubbling and spewing out gouts of sulphur. It made Lewis feel prickly, a feeling which grew worse when he heard the hollow, empty tone of her voice. "You want me to be nice to you? You killed my girl friend and Joe Forrest, you carried me away by force and you want me to be nice? Lewis, you're insane."

So, thought Lewis, she thought Carol was dead. That could work to his advantage if she wanted to become defiant.

"Did you love that boat shyster?" he asked.

"He was a pleasant man. But I didn't love him."

He lowered himself to the grass and leaned back against the bank. He was enjoying the delay now, knowing that whenever he chose to take her, there would be nothing to stop him. It gave him a feeling of power.

"Did you love your husband?"

"I love my husband," she said quietly, emphasizing the present tense.

"Yet, I was the one who saved your life."

She glared at him and spat, "I wish I'd died!"

He met her eyes until she looked away.

"Get up," he said.

She didn't move.

He flicked the safety of the gun. "I said get up."

Still she sat, and he felt his annoyance building into a rage.

"You think I won't shoot? Is that it? Because I'm afraid of being heard? Damn! You know how many guns are fired every day in these woods? Squirrel season is year-'round, rabbit season too. Who's going to chase off after a gunshot? So get up! Get up!"

He was standing in front of her when he finished, punctuating his words with jabs of the gun. She sat looking down, tracing a pattern in the grass with her finger.

With a great effort he kept his voice calm and even. "Anyway, what makes you think I'd use a gun? I killed a girl once with a towel wrapped around her neck. That was years ago. Night before last I killed a girl with a rock."

She stiffened, but didn't look up. He seized her hair and bent her back. "You believe me?"

Again he found himself looking into the pit of hatred.

"Yes," she said. "I believe you."

"Then what's your answer?"

Her mouth puckered, then he felt the warm cottony saliva strike his cheekbone and spatter over his face. His action was reflexive; he swung his free hand and struck her face with his open palm. She sprawled on the ground, her hair spilling over her face.

Lewis straightened and wiped his cheek with his sleeve. He looked down at the woman and smiled slowly. She was smart, he decided. She knew he wouldn't kill her before he enjoyed her. And in some strange way, her act of spitting on him had been intimate and exciting...

Now what? He could take her by force, sure; there'd be an exhilarating struggle with a foregone conclusion. But it wasn't exactly what he wanted. He wanted complete power over her, the kind you can exercise without using your muscles. And he thought he knew a way to get it.

"You don't care if I kill you, is that it?" he asked softly.

"I don't care," came her muffled voice.

"How about your daughter?"

Her head came up like that of a doe scenting danger.

"My daughter?"

"You've sent her away," he said gently. "But I could find her."

"You wouldn't—"

"I'd kill her."

"She's only twelve!"

He smiled. "That first girl I told you about was thirteen."

She stared at him for a moment, the fear bright in her eyes. Then her body sagged like a bundle of old clothes. She pushed herself to her feet and stood with her shoulders drooping.

"What do you want me to do?"

He smiled and sat down with his back against the bank, stretching his feet out in front of him.

"Undress," he said. "Slowly."

Her fingers fumbled at the buttons of the blouse. She peeled it away from her damp flesh and dropped it on the grass. She reached back and unhooked the bra, then humped her shoulders forward and let it slide down her arms, catching the cups in her hands. Her eyes were downcast.

"Go on," he said, "but look at me."

She raised her eyes to his and he saw that they no longer held hatred. They held nothing. They were the eyes of someone dead, blank and empty, like holes drilled into her skull.

Lewis watched her loosen the skirt and let it fall to her feet. She stepped out of its circle, then hooked her thumbs in her panties.

"Slowly," he said.

She obeyed, and Lewis watched the white wisp of nylon drift slowly down the brown thighs like a flag of surrender. And yet, he thought, the flesh there is no different from the flesh of a woman's thumb or her earlobe. Yet who fondles her thumb, and who desires her earlobe? Nobody. They are available, they can be had for the taking. Yes, that's the reason; this part is desired because it is hidden, because it is hoarded and doled to men in return for their favors ...

Now he understood it all. In the beginning, this little commodity was a lure to keep the man close to the cave, to keep him bringing in those nice warm mammoth skins. Then it was rationed and reserved for the man whose chariot ran in the money, or the man who returned from the crusades with rich loot from the Levant. Now it went to the man who provided the Levittown home, the insurance premiums and charge accounts and the washer-dryer combinations. The price of this tiny tuft of flesh was being driven up year after year. And the women were outsmarting themselves; by making this commodity so scarce, they had blown up its value beyond reason, and so the women of the world created the rapist.

The thought made him laugh. They created me! He saw that Marian was standing nude in a patch of sunlight slanting down through the trees. It struck each breast with its rose-pink tip rising up like a surprised exclamation point.

"You created me," he told her. "You know that?"

She looked at him without expression.

"You have nobody to blame but yourself. You didn't have to be in this position. You could have given me what I wanted."

Still she did not react. It was no use. She was a puppet, geared to his orders. She no longer moved on her own initiative, only on his. He smiled at the idea and decided to test it.

"Straighten your shoulders," he said abruptly.

Her shoulders came back, her breasts rose up and lay on the pectoral flatness of her chest.

"Pull in your stomach."

The flat plane of her stomach became a scooped-out hollow; her navel diminished to a tiny hole; her pelvis caught the sun, casting a fuzzy shadow on her thigh.

"Now walk around," he said.

She took a hesitant step, then paused. "Walk?"

"Walk," he said. "Till I tell you to stop."

She began a slow, measured pacing in front of him, from one end of the little meadow to the other, then back again. She never looked at him, but he knew she was totally conscious of his gaze. It showed in the tight, frozen blankness of her face and in the awkward flat-heeled way she walked. There was no spring to her knees, her belly jiggled with each step, her breasts dipped and bounced upward, her buttocks thrust and stretched.

Lewis watched her move and pondered another riddle. What is a woman? Beneath the surface of those sweat-gleaming breasts lies a maze of tissues and glands that serve only one purpose; to feed the young. And beneath the trembling satin stomach are miles of gnarled and twisted tubing tangled like fishworms in a can; there is the blue elastic sack of a stomach which stretches and contracts and gurgles, and beneath the soft curve of her back nestle the kidneys like two little coin purses...

Yes, he thought, these things are women—strung together on a frame of bones, held up by muscle in a coat of skin and directed by a blob of gray tissues stuffed in behind the eyes.

This is Marian, the woman I risked so much to get. For a moment he hated her for being a woman, for being flesh and blood like all the others, an animal that sweats and cries and defecates and eats and sleeps ... and dies.

"Walk toward me," he said. "Slowly."

She was ten feet away when he spoke. She turned

and came toward him, placing one foot carefully before the other. He raised the gun. He could stop it now, turn this flesh cold forever. He could shoot her in the trembling stomach; she would stop suddenly, grunt in surprise, and the hole would appear on her flesh, blip! An instant blemish, white-rimmed and swollen around the edge, black, black at the center where it led the eye to the inside.

"Stop," he said. She was a foot away, and her odor came to him, an odor of sweat and ... what? Yes, hate. The hate was a sour acridity which made his nostrils tingle. He liked it.

"Lie down," he said.

She dropped slowly to her knees in front of him, sank back on her haunches, then swung her legs out in front of her and lay back on the grass.

Lewis stood and gazed down at her. Her eyes were fixed blankly on a point straight overhead.

"This is what we started so long ago," he said, smiling. "How do you feel?"

She cleared her throat. "The grass ... tickles my back."

"I'd like it better if you enjoyed it."

Her eyes turned toward him, then widened. She drew a deep breath, licked her lips, and then gave him a tremulous smile.

"If you say so, Lewis."

He was pleased, but mildly surprised. "Can you?"

"I ... think so. I was tired of that stupid walking, Lewis." Her tongue came out and ran over her lips. "It's no fun to walk. I'd welcome a change."

"You ... would?"

"You're slow, Lewis. Awfully slow."

He stared down at her, not quite believing his eyes. She was running her palms over her stomach, pulling at her flesh, twisting her thighs, lifting herself up until he could see the ground beneath her buttocks ...

He felt the blood throb against his temples. God, all this time he had been doing it wrong. If he had used this at the beginning, there would have been no need for the cave, no need to wait so long...

He fumbled at his belt and found one hand occupied by his gun. He set it carefully out of Marian's reach. He was not sure of her yet. Then he reached out and ...

He got no warning, except for a brief flicker in Marian's eyes. Lewis felt a sudden searing pain in his shoulder. He was jerked backward off his feet: cold metal bit into his shoulder, ripping through the muscles, tearing the blood vessels, drenching him with hot blood. His back thumped on the ground. He thought, That's why she came on so strong, to get me off guard ...

A voice boomed from above.

"God damn you! If you move I'll rip your throat out."

Lewis opened his eyes to see Dee towering over him. Dee had a fishing gaff five inches from Lewis' throat, its point still dripping blood. Lewis moved and felt an excruciating pain ...

"What you gonna do?" he croaked.

"I'll see you executed, Lewis. If I can't do that I'll see you put away in a nut house the rest of your lousy life."

"No, Dee!" Lewis recognized Marian's voice, and Lewis felt a surge of surprise. Good God, I didn't expect her to plead for me.

He saw her come up to stand beside her husband, still with her body unadorned. His eyes widened. She held the gun in both hands, and pointed it directly at him. Her fingers whitened on the trigger.

He twisted as the gun went off. The bullets smashed his hip, and rolled him over. He could feel the shattered slivers of bone piercing the flesh around his hip. She was aiming the gun again, her eyes narrowed to slits. Her husband was watching her in horror. Everything seemed to happen in slow motion, but Lewis was too weak to move. The second bullet thumped into his chest, feeling like a huge rock which had been dropped from a great height. Something warm and fluid spread through his insides. He tried to breathe but the hot syrupy liquid filled his windpipe and choked him.

The third bullet tore through his throat, but it was no worse than a sudden, sharp tingle, for the darkness was already gathering in his brain. The fourth bullet ripped into his heart, and he didn't feel that one at all...

Marian felt as though she were in a pit full of swirling fire. Little red-eyed animals were trying to seize her in their claws and tear her flesh, and all she had to fight with was a tiny little stick. There were thousands, and they kept coming ... more of them, more of them.

Dee's voice penetrated the red fire. "Marian! Stop! He's dead! He's dead! Stop!"

She felt his hands gripping her shoulders, pulling her off some strange shape.

"He's dead, Marian. Don't look at him."

But she did, then quickly turned away from the grotesque, reddened thing on the ground. She felt a weight in her hand and saw the gun, smeared with blood.

She threw it from her as though it were a dead, slimy creature. She bent to wipe her hands on the grass and nausea overcame her. She doubled over and tasted sour bile. Her stomach knotted and spewed up its contents. Dee was there with his arm beneath her shoulders, his hand on her forehead. Finally the retching ended. She straightened, felt her knees go weak, and fell against him. Her brow was dewed with cold sweat. His arms were around her and his hand stroked her hair.

"Dee," she gasped. "What did I do?"

"You emptied the gun in him. Then you started hitting him with the gun."

His words were calm and gentle, but each one brought a new twitch of nausea to her stomach. "Why didn't you stop me?"

"I was too shocked. Then..." She felt his shrug. "After the first two shots it didn't matter. You had to make sure he was dead. So he wouldn't come back for you. You had to do it yourself, I suppose, or you wouldn't really believe it."

He held her around the waist and started picking up her clothing.

"We'll get away from here. You can forget this."

He took her down the hill and stopped beneath a tree. He held out her clothes. "Better dress. Someone might come."

She took the clothes and stared at him; his rugged face had never looked so good to her. She stuck her feet into her panties and pulled them up. She felt better, now that she'd left the scene. "You know, when I first saw you, I was so damned happy—I never thought you'd find us."

"I'm not a bad tracker. And I heard him laugh."

"But you waited up there so long ... I kept walking, and wondering how I could keep from showing it."

"I couldn't risk anything while he had that damn gun on you." He looked at her, disturbed for a moment. "That's why you did that last? Lay down so readily..."

"Dee! What other reason?"

He looked thoughtful, then nodded. "Okay. No questions."

She pulled on her skirt and fastened it. Suddenly she thought of something that filled her eyes with tears. "Dee, I just remembered Carol and Joe!"

"Carol is okay. Joe's hurt, but he'll recover."

"Oh, God!" Joy flooded through her, so strong that she dropped her bra and threw her arms around his neck. "Dee! Then everything is all—Oh, no. Sharon."

"She'll be all right."

"But she heard about me—"

"We'll think of something logical to tell her later."

"And you—?"

"I ask nothing. I'm satisfied just to have you." He put his arms around her and she felt his lips against her.

THE END

CHARLES RUNYON BIBLIOGRAPHY
(1928-2015)

The Anatomy of Violence (1960)
Color Him Dead (1963, reprinted as *The Incarnate*, 1977)
The Death Cycle (1963)
The Prettiest Girl I Ever Killed (1965)
The Black Moth (1967)
No Place to Hide (1970)
Power Kill (1972)
Something Wicked (unpublished, 1973) [aka *Dorian-7*, scheduled to be published by Lancer Books before they went out of business]
To Kill a Dead Man (1976) [aka A Killer is a Lonely Man; author's title]

As Charles Runyon Jr.
Gypsy King (1979)

As Charles W. Runyon
The Bloody Jungle (1966)
Pigworld (1971)
Ames Holbrook, Deity (1972)
I, Weapon (1974)
Soulmate (1974)
Kiss the Girls and Make Them Die (1977)

As Ellery Queen
The Last Score (1964)
The Killer Touch (1965)
Kiss and Kill (1969)

As Mark West
Office Affair (1961)
His Boss's Wife (1962)
Object of Lust (1962)

BIOGRAPHY

Charles Runyon was born June 9, 1928 in Sheridan, Missouri, and after studying at various universities, worked as an editor for oil companies. He began writing fiction in the mid-50's, primarily for the men's magazines, and produced over 20 novels. He was nominated for the Edgar Allan Poe award of the MWA for *Power Kill*. Runyon is also known for his dystopic science fiction, as well as three ghost-written Ellery Queen novels. He died on June 8, 2015, in Cedar Park, Texas.

Black Gat Books is a new line of mass market paperbacks introduced in 2015 by Stark House Press. New titles appear every other month, featuring the best in crime fiction reprints. Each book is size to 4.25" x 7", just like they used to be. Collect them all.

Harry Whittington · A Haven for the Damned #1 ·

Charlie Stella · Eddie's World #2

Leigh Brackett · Stranger at Home #3

John Flagg · The Persian Cat #4

Malcolm Braly · Felony Tank #6

Vin Packer 8 The Girl on the Best Seller List #7

Orrie Hitt · She Got What She Wanted #8

Helen Nielsen · The Woman on the Roof #9

Lou Cameron · Angel's Flight #10

Gary Lovisi · The Affair of Lady Westcott's Lost Ruby / The Case of the Unseen Assassin #11

Arnold Hano · The Last Notch #12

Clifton Adams · Never Say No to a Killer #13

Ed Lacy · The Men From the Boys #14

Henry Kane · Frenzy of Evil #15

William Ard · You'll Get Yours #16

Bert & Dolores Hitchens · End of the Line #17

Noël Calef · Frantic #18

Ovid Demaris · The Hoods Take Over #19

Fredric Brown · Madball #20

Louis Malley Stool Pigeon #21

Frank Kane · The Living End #22

Ferguson Findley · My Old Man's Badge #23

Paul Connolly · Tears are for Angels #24

E. P. Fenwick · Two Names for Death #25

Lorenz Heller · Dead Wrong #26

Robert Martin · Little Sister #27

Calvin Clements · Satan Takes the Helm #28

Jack Karney · Cut Me In #29

George Benet · The Hoodlums #30

Jonathan Craig · So Young, So Wicked #31

Edna Sherry · Tears for Jessie Hewitt #32

William O'Farrell · Repeat Performance #33

Marvin Albert · The Girl With No Place to Hide #34

Edward S. Aarons · Gang Rumble #35

William Fuller · Back Country #36

Robert Silverberg · The Killer #37

William R. Cox · Make My Coffin Strong #38

A. S. Fleischman · Blood Alley #39

Harold R. Daniels · The Girl in 304 #40

William H. Duhart - The Deadly Pay-Off #41

Robert Ames - Awake and Die #42

Stark House Press
1315 H Street, Eureka, CA 95501 (707) 498-3135
griffinskye3@sbcglobal.net www.starkhousepress.com
Available from your local bookstore or direct from the publisher

www.ingramcontent.com/pod-product-compliance
Lightning Source LLC
LaVergne TN
LVHW021825060526
838201LV00058B/3515